Distant Worlds

DISTANT WORLDS

Distant Worlds

Cover illustrated by Jennie Elaine

For more excellent works of fiction, visit Inkandquill-press.com

Table of Contents

1

Black Angel - Jennie Elaine

Tori LeBlanc had the kind of kitchen table you'd find in a pile of unwanted trash from Earth-side twice as old as she was. It was in too poor of a shape to call it retro; the yellow tabletop was pockmarked with scratches and cigarette burns, the ribbed metal edging ranged from rust to black patina, and the odd steel legs were dinged and misshapen. She'd propped a stack of brown-stained playing cards under one to keep it even.

The trailer had an odd hum in the air, lacking the stillness I'd come to expect from the down and lonely corners of the world. You saw plenty of those, spending a lifetime chasing after Donner Mayberry. You learned the taste of stagnant, drugged-up air and city sewers and the emptiness where someone used to reside. Homes became houses the moment their owners died, either in soul or body. Mayberry had made a career of taking one or both from everyone in his path.

Tori LeBlanc, for a change of pace, was only dying in body. Her spirit was still very much alive.

She only had one chair—a metal folding contraption that was almost too short—and was occupying it, so I leaned my hip against the counter. A tight pinch of pain came from the broken laminate edge, but I made no motion to move.

Despite sitting well below my eye level and in a seat she barely fit, Tori felt larger than me, and when her blue eyes looked at me I felt I was the one looking up to meet them.

I knew why I was there. I knew what I wanted. I had yet to figure out why she'd entertained me, a dangerous lapse of knowledge.

"Sorry to make you wait, honey," said the retired star at last, the first words she had spoken to me since I'd entered her trailer home and she'd smoked half a cig, "but if you're here to ask me about him, I needed this first."

"Nicotine does keep you young." It was something my mother had said to me back when I used to speak to her. Last I'd seen her, she'd become just another junkie who looked a decade older than she was. Tori also fit into that strange valley of agelessness. Looking at her, she could be anywhere between her rough thirties or her glowing fifties, and I'd lose money on whichever I bet. From smoking or running with Mayberry in her youth, I couldn't tell.

Tori was thin to the point of bone definition, with closely shaved gray-blonde hair that looked nearly transparent in the light. Her cheekbones and jawline cut harsh edges around a face lined with age and smoothed with a light dusting of perfectly applied foundation, blue eyeshadow, and thick mascara. Despite the attempt at glamor, she still looked so very, very tired. Her voice ran like glass through a garbage disposal but lilted like a flute, and when she waved her cigarette hand, it made her low-dangling topaz statement earrings swing.

I had caught her that morning in a sheer gray tank that hung off of cut collarbones and some well-loved flannel pajama bottoms. Her feet were bare, and like her hands the nails were painted a perfect robin's egg blue.

Tori laughed. It was a shocked cackle that filled the room and pushed the morning light back a few paces. The empty wine bottle on the table shook. For a moment the hung photos of a smiling Tori in younger years and better dress seemed to come to life, filling scenes of lunar bars and velvet-curtained stages with the same amazing sound. It was over soon and she dabbed the corners of her eyes, minding the makeup.

"Oh honey," she smiled, pointing her long fingers at me. "If I'm young then you must be an infant. A little babe playing dress up in your leather loafers and big city suit. Save whatever cover story you've concocted to get in my door: you look the part, hun, but I can smell the gutter on you from a mile away."

I should have been surprised. Guilty, even. I wasn't.

"Is that why you let me in despite working so hard to stay hidden?" I asked, my fingers running over the item in my pocket as they had since I first walked into the cramped kitchen.

"Honey," tutted the ex-lover of the most wanted man from Earth to moonside, "gutter rats have always been my people. Like calls to like, after all."

For a gutter rat in an antiquated trailer, Tori sure kept the place spotless. The counters were cluttered with spices, mixers, and blenders, but there were no spills. The sink was clear of dishes, and the glass front cabinets were stocked but organized. The floor was laminate that cracked and curled away from the wall, but the well-loved broom and mop in the corner told her own story of use.

No matter where I looked, expecting roach leavings or worse, all I got was the feeling that this home, like its owner, had much more to it than first met the eye.

Retired, yes, but still a goddess nonetheless. A star, once.

God, how far she'd fallen.

"If you know what I am," I told her, "then you know why I'm here. I'm willing to pay for your time and information."

"Honey," she chided me like a child and not the grown man I was so tired of being. "I have all the riches I could ever ask for. I have a home full of memories and a body riddled with death," she paused again to take a long drag off of her cigarette. Her voice turned bitter. "Funny how things work, isn't it? Decades with that man, running his drugs from this end of the lunar coastal ports to that end of the dark-side alleys by the skin of my teeth and it's a fucking cancer that's dragging me to hell. We used to be gods, honey. Gods. Unstoppable highs at the cost of the lowest lows, the lunar marshals in our pockets, and a moon at our feet, and I'm getting dropped by human sickness."

Tori's laughter turned into a dark, horrid thing—and for the briefest of moments, I saw her as she'd once been; ethereal, high on the stars, and as dark as the spaces between them. I saw the touch of Donner Mayberry within them and saw how stained her very bones were with his essence. My hand tightened around the vial in my pocket, grounding me against the insight.

It's better to be dead than to carry his sins. The only thing worse, I knew, was surviving after others were buried because of his actions.

Tori looked at me once more, both of us falling into ourselves in the present. Her eyes, so bright and pale, were sharper than any knife I could have hidden on my body, and I'd brought plenty.

"Save your money. My bank account is secondary honey, secondary."

"Fine," I said as if I understood, "then what comes first?"

At this Tori turned away, propping her elbow on the table and glancing off into some place I couldn't see. Her eyes mulled over the question as she took a long, deliberate pull from the last inch of her cigarette.

"The same thing I have so foolishly wanted my whole damned life," she finally said around a mouthful of smoke. Like a vice, her eyes grabbed mine. "To claim even a single ounce of Donner Mayberry as mine."

I had nothing to say to that. Why anyone would want any part of that monster was far beyond me.

"When I was young and stupid," she began suddenly, "an equally young but far less stupid Donner Mayberry shot a man point blank for me and I fell so, so foolishly in love."

I waited for more. She didn't offer it. "Why?' I prompted.

"I wasn't brought up with a silver spoon," she continued, "I started the same as any low-born lunar trash; I was the daughter of some worthless man Earth expelled off-planet and the woman who took his money for a quick fuck. Grew up on the southern edge of the Grimaldi port where my mom could earn her credits. Left that shithole for a new one as soon as I could."

She put another cigarette between her lips. I reached out with the old golden lighter I always carried with me. She stared at its sapphire embeds for a moment too long before closing her eyes and leaning into the flame. I didn't wait for her to begin again.

"Where did you go?"

"Skipped up north to Copernicus."

"Why there?"

"You know how inclusive the pleasure dens in Grimaldi are." She moved her cigarette in a circle, pointing at me, "I wasn't gifted the same parts between my legs my mother was. I had to buy those myself, far later. They only allowed born women to work the port dens, and I wasn't desperate enough to try my luck further out. I'd seen what befell any-one unfortunate enough to work at the edges of the atmos-phere generators. And I was in love."

"Mayberry?" I asked.

She snorted. "No, the man he killed for me. Jack. Same old story you hear a hundred times; a man twice my age promised me this world and that one–" she pointed upwards towards her ceiling where, had we been outside, the vast visage of Earth would have occupied our sky. "And all I had to do was move up north with him. The part I was too stupid and naive to hear was *and away from anyone who would protect you.*"

I didn't have much to add. I'd heard similar stories my entire miserable life. Seen what a determined and desperate person could gain from manipulating a lover, and had also witnessed the fallout for either side. I didn't need cheap tricks to make my way on Lune, only a gun and my own name.

"You look down on my life now, but you should have seen me then," she snorted, lost in a memory. "Turns out even 240,000 miles away from Earth, men are all the same."

"But not Mayberry." A statement, not a question.

She looked at an empty photo frame on the wall to her right. The frame was old, real wood and cracked diagonally like it had been thrown against a wall many times. The picture, whatever it had been, was long gone. "Where men had failed me," she answered honestly, "a God appeared in an alley, shot Jack between the lungs, and extended his hand towards me. All because he'd heard me sing for a few credits that night and saw something in me no one else had. He called it potential. How was I going to say no?"

"What did the Reaper of Lune want with some bar singer?"

"He wasn't the reaper back then, child. He was still climbing his way out of the craters, some nobody from nowhere with the mind of a king and two worlds he planned to exploit. He and his gang, small as they were in the beginning, had been working to synthesize a new kind of drug for the market; one that was twice as addictive as anything else out there and three times as profitable. They'd been selling it to the lower borns but Don wanted to aim higher, said the real money was in the spaceports with the tourists that could get their fix and take it back home to their rich Earth buddies. They just needed a way in."

I knew about her career. Everyone did. "He built you up as a high end act," I guessed, "Sold your voice on stage and started selling at the shows."

"Absolutely," she pushed out, breathless with pride at Mayberry's genius. "And it worked. Not only to get the drug out and fill our pockets, but to get my name out there, to push me higher and higher into the world other men had only promised me, and all the while there he was, keeping those promises and more. He took a girl off the streets and built her an empire." Her face softened, her eyes flashing with a brightness I didn't expect her capable of still having. "And when we'd both made names for ourselves, on the last day of my first official lunar tour, I claimed him backstage and clung on for dear life."

"He used you."

"And in doing so he made me," she countered, "He was a genius. He'd always seen Lune for what it was; a prison in everything but name. He'd always said that prisons ran on their own laws, so he'd long stopped playing by society's rules."

"Criminals rarely do."

"Successful criminals never do," she said. "You want to get anywhere in a prison? You find a way to be worth something to everyone around you, and then you hang on tight. No mercy for those that would tear you down, no reliance on anyone else. Just yourself."

"I know the story of his rise," I said. Everyone does.

"You don't know what it was like to share a bed with him when he did it," she purred.

I didn't want to.

Tori continued. "By the time demand began to outpace the supply, he was prepared for what he needed to do. City by city, with the strategy of a general and the results of a warlord, he tore down all competitor drug runners with his teeth, blew up any distribution points that weren't advantageous, and took over the ones that were. He had his men in the labs mass-producing Black Angel long before it even had a name or we had a place to put it. Within months, half of Lune was in his pockets or under his thumb, we had labs for production, warehouses to store it, and ports to ship it en masse to Earth."

"An empire built on addicts."

"Gold is still gold," she mused, "no matter who paid for it."

"Ms. LeBlanc," I asked, my patience wearing thin. "Where is he?"

Tori stared at the lit end of her cigarette, her other hand running across the short stubble of her hair. "I loved him, you know."

"If he loved you back," I retorted, "then how did you end up in some shithole on the lower side of Byrgeius, dying alone and forgotten?"

Tori didn't answer for a long, long time. "In a prison," she whispered, "you're only allowed to climb as high as the wardens allow you."

"That doesn't answer my question."

"He grew tired of me," she snapped. "He left me for another woman. Someone we'd long been friends with, some high-maintenance floozy who refused to smoke if her cigarette wasn't lit with a golden lighter, or eat if not from a golden spoon, and who was born with the right parts to grant him an heir."

"He was a fool," I said simply, "she was an agent for Earth's law, paid outside of the Marshal's crooked influence."

"So we all figured out," she said, "far too late. By then she'd already tied himself into the operations with his child. Things started to fall apart. Earth's law began to pull us apart from the inside. Anyone who wasn't taken into custody scattered into the winds, or fell from grace with no recourse." She tapped one nail against the table twice for herself. "He held on for so long, refusing to believe it was her...I heard she lost her mind after he found out. Earth refused to take her in like they'd promised and left her to rot, addicted to Black Angel like the rest of them."

She'd heard correctly.

"Where is he?" I demanded again.

"How bad is his empire now," she asked me, "that in his absence you've hunted me down to find him? You must have exhausted every other avenue to end up in my kitchen."

"New lower moon lords are rising again," I answered honestly, desperate to push her into giving me what I needed. "The Marshals are taking bribes outside of the Reaper's pockets. Everyone is scrambling to take his throne, but with no idea where he is, it's chaos. A free for all, every wannabe gang leader for himself."

"So nothing new than the world he'd started with."

"Innocents are dying," I snapped, slamming a hand on her shitty table.

She laughed at me, dark and bitter once more, "There are no innocents on Lune."

"There's no order," I continued, "Only chaos, and without Donner Mayberry dead or at the helm, the name of the Reaper means nothing. He built a world and abandoned it to rot as soon as it wasn't fun anymore."

"Is that why you want to find him?" she pressed, "to kill him, make a name for yourself, and be top of the heap?"

"I want to find him," I told her between my teeth, "because when he decided to abandon his post, and there was no one for his enemies to point their guns at, they turned them to anyone even remotely close to Donner Mayberry and pulled the fucking trigger."

She paused, narrowing her eyes at me. "You never told me. What wannabe gang lord are you?"

This, I refused to answer. I didn't need to. She'd known who I was the moment I'd shown up at her door.

"Fine, then." She settled, "Who did you lose?"

I almost didn't answer. But her name slipped from my lips before I could pull it back. "Her name was Deserae."

She looked at the two rings on my left hand, one on my index finger and the smaller one on my pinkie. "Your wife?"

"She should have been."

If I was expecting her eyes to turn sad, or remorse, or pitying, I'd learned nothing about Tori LeBlanc. Her shoulders fell back, all the fight leaving her only to be replaced with a deep, bone-weary sadness.

"We've really made a mess of things, haven't we?" she asked the empty picture frame. To me, she said, "If you're gonna make something out of this world again, bring back the stages. Find someone young and beautiful and broken, and give them the spotlight they deserve. And when they fall," she added, looking up to me with shaking red lips, "let it be in splendor until the very end."

I looked at her, all of her, and could only nod.

She told me if I was to look anywhere for Donner Mayberry, to start Earthside. "He'd always wanted to own a bar," she said, "retire somewhere quiet by the sea. He said Sicily had the most beautiful oceans. I said I'd paint the front door to match the color of the waves, and we could retire together."

The empty dreams of a foolish girl, in love with glamor and the man who'd given it to her.

"Thank you," I answered honestly, not shying away from the tears that now spilled down her face. I couldn't begin to imagine what reliving all of this meant to her, how deep the knife stuck in and twisted with every word she spilled.

"I don't want your thanks," she snapped through the tears, refusing to look my way. "I only want you to finish what you came here to achieve. Tell that man the ugly, crumpled husk that'll be left of me when I die, will see him at the gates of hell, and you be sure to let him know who sent him there."

I stepped across the room, my tailored shoes loud in the silence. I pulled the lone vial out of my pocket and set it on her tiny, shitty table. It thrummed at a heartbeat's pace between us.

"You still keep a fix kit?" I asked her, those wicked blue eyes now latched onto the glass tube between us.

"Somewhere around here," she barely answered me, reaching to take it off the table and hold it up to the light. She observed the oil-slick black liquid inside like it was gold. Ounce per ounce, it sold for more than gold anyway. I'd brought her about three ounces of the stuff; a small fortune. "This is actually top-shelf, isn't it?"

"Third-generation mix," I replied, "The kind even Earth is falling over themselves to stop. Three drops of this is a full dose. Six will have you in the stratosphere for a week. Half of that vial will kill you."

She was silent for a long heartbeat. Then her lips breathed out one simple word.

"Why?"

"Because I promised an old family friend that I would find someone young, and beautiful, and broken, and give them the spotlight they deserve. Thank you," I said once more, and this time she didn't refuse me. She couldn't move, didn't speak. Her eyes never left the small, innocuous vial between her manicured fingers.

"You look so much like her, you know," came the last words Tori LeBlanc ever spoke to me when I turned to close her trailer door, "Your mother, I mean."

I stared at the proud, frail form before me, and then I left.

~~~

The image of Tori LeBlanc's body made headlines before my feet touched ground Earthside.

She'd died as she should have lived; on her terms, vibrantly beautiful, and immortalized by the very drug that had made her who she was.

Lunar Star with Ties to Reaper Dead by Overdose, read the more modest headlines. 'Godmother of Black Angel' Dead by her Own Sins declared the rest. Ding dong, they seemed to proclaim, the wicked witch is dead. Others cried at such a tragic fall from grace as if they could ever understand she'd hit the ground on her own terms.

I caught the photo on every screen in sight. She'd been stunning. The perfect visage of the woman she'd been in her prime. She'd shaved her legs, repainted her nails a glittering black, adorned a backless vermillion dress, and a styled blonde wig half pinned in delicate braids and half down in floor-length curls.
~~~

She'd fallen forward, her black gold heels scattered across the very stage she'd sang on for Donner Mayberry all those years ago, her face turned to the side and her ribs and lungs blown out with the force of an entire vial of Black Angel. Donner Mayberry had marketed it for the high, but the overdose death it caused was what had stuck for a name. The spray of blood and ichor from her body gave her spread black wings large enough to fly away from this awful world.

Her face was serene, a smile on her painted lips—a death befitting a goddess.

I found a bar by the waters called Diavulu. The day was heading into mid-afternoon when I walked up to a wooden door painted the same sparkling green as the ocean around me, the street silent hours before the bar crowd would come.

Donner Mayberry, though, was never one to rest. I stepped into the open door and found him sitting at his bartop, facing away from me, the only soul in this miserable place.

Age had caught up to him at last. Grey hair crept past his dark chestnut temples and banded around his head, turning his shoulder-length style into a streaky mess of silver and brown. His hands were beginning to wrinkle, the skin looking thinner in places. His shoulders still carried bulk, his stance tilted with the tell-tale signs of a dangerous man, and yet he was in a simple white button-down and beer-stained work khakis. A far cry from the immaculate suits I had grown up knowing him in.

I'd already pulled out my gun, one purchased shortly after landing. Earth had always preferred we bought their guns if us Lune-born bastards were going to come down here and cause trouble.

In front of him, I saw the same photo of Tori's body, printed out in full color on actual paper. There was no technology in sight, even the registers were antiques that consisted of little more than a drawer for cash and buttons to count it all up. Beside that was an empty glass of whiskey.

"You're the one who gave it to her, then," he said to my shadow, falling across his drink and photo.

"I had to thank her somehow," I answered honestly, steadying the weapon in both hands, "for finally giving you up."

"She was always the brightest star in my night's sky," he said, not bothering to move his back away from me. I had no delusions that he hadn't been expecting me, or that he wasn't aware of the gun I now held level with his skull.

"Save me your bullshit," I told him flatly, "You let her reach those same stars then kicked out the ladder and ran. Same as my mother, same as your empire. Lune's fell into turf wars and hell without you there. The quality of your product is cut again and again by pissants who think they have a claim at the game. You've set an entire moon up to fall."

"I did love her, you know." He spoke as if he hadn't heard me. "A long time ago. Leaving her was my first and worst mistake."

"She deserved better," I told the place on his skull where my gun aimed, "They all deserved better."

He let his cigarette ash fall down his knuckles, not moving to flick it away. "Did they? Everyone on that damned moon is just as guilty of their actions as I am, Raleigh." He snorted, not quite a laugh. "Hell, you've made quite a name for yourself up on Lune. The Demon's Shadow, you know they call you? I heard about your rampage through Plato after your little girlfriend died."

My hand did not waiver. "I've made a name for myself cleaning up your messes."

"You think you'll do any better than me?"

"I already am."

He took one last drink from the glass before him. "How nice it must be, to have not made the mistakes I have—yet."

Yet. I tightened my jaw. "It all comes back to you."

"And now it ends with you."

I didn't hesitate. "Yes."

He took his last drag from his cigarette, a thin trail of smoke rising from his lips. His other hand traced a slow, gentle line down Ms. Tori LeBlanc's photographed face, almost like a caress.

"Take care of the empire, son."

I tightened my finger on the trigger.

"I'll see you in hell, Dad."

2

The Source - Ian Withrow

"Miranda, this is control, how are we looking?"

Miranda was chewing on her lip, her brow furrowed in concentration as she focused on steadying her trembling hands.

"I'm fine control, just… just being extra cautious."

"Roger, take your time Captain."

She rolled her eyes, but out here there was no one to see it.

Take your time, Captain. No worries, Captain. The whole world is watching, Captain.

She bit her tongue though, in no small part because she knew every word would be recorded and memorialized for all time.

She took a glance at the heads-up display projected on her helmet's visor. Aside from slightly elevated heart rate and blood pressure readings, everything was green.

She let out part of the breath she was holding, then focused in on her hands again. She was still holding the long braided polymer cable that connected her to her only lifeline. She looked back over her shoulder at the Herald, which she'd landed about sixty yards away. She could see the cord, and all of the anchor points she'd placed so far along her trek were secure.

The small landing pod was scarcely big enough for the measuring equipment it carried, let alone the sole occupant expected to travel down to the surface with it. But beyond it, hovering silent in the void of space, was the vast bulk of the Ascendant, the pride of the United Planetary Navy's research fleet. Sleek lines and polished white bulkheads reassured her that she was far from alone out here, despite how it felt inside her tiny space suit.

She returned to her work, retrieving another alloy stake from the toolbox she'd brought with her. She clipped her tether into the loop of the stake and then set it against the rocky surface of the asteroid beneath her feet.

After ensuring that her mag-boots were set to maximum strength, she swung the heavy tungsten hammer she carried. The impact drove the stake in easily, while nearly lifting her from the surface. Thankfully, her boots held. She gave the stake a firm tug and, when it refused to budge, bent to retrieve her tools and instruments.

"Control, this is Miranda. Stake six embedded, proceeding to target."

"Roger, good copy."

Minutes ticked by in silence as she worked her way painstakingly across the harsh, rocky surface. Yard by yard, stake by stake, she made her way to what her team had dubbed 'the entrance.'

Finally, she'd made it. A short distance before her stretched a perfectly circular void in the rock. She looked at the lip of the hole as she drew nearer and was in awe of the razor sharp, impossibly precise edge. Her in-suit sensors did a quick scan of the opening and confirmed what she already knew. The circle was perfect, variance was 0.00% along the entire shape. No mortal instrument could have crafted such perfection, she'd seen laser drills less precise.

She activated her mapping software and a wire diagram projected itself over the hole, measuring its diameter and depth in an instant. It was 31.4 feet across and... that couldn't be right.

Her diagnostics weren't giving her a stable depth reading. The number simply kept growing until it blanked out.

eRR.

She rebooted the program.

eRR.

"Uh, control, I'm getting some odd readings here."

"We're tracking, captain, running shipboard diagnostics on your suit. Standby"

Standby.

Miranda quirked an eyebrow, what else was she going to do, pack it in? She was by herself on a rock floating in outer space. Of course she was going to stand by.

"Suit is reading green across the board, you're good to proceed."

She took a deep, unsteady breath.

"Roger, good copy control."

Miranda closed the last few feet and was greeted at last with the reason they'd come all this way. The hole emitted a pale blue light that washed over her as she leaned out over the edge. Not so far as to risk falling, but enough to get a good look.

Instantly her suit's communications suite spiked. Every band, every channel, every signal that humanity had learned to listen for jumped clear off the charts. Tiny alert lights and warning indicators populated her heads-up display, prompting her to take a few steps back. They quieted instantly.

This was it then, The Source.

Fifty-four years ago, before the United Planetary Navy was even a pipe dream, humanity had suddenly and loudly been informed that they weren't alone. At 7:31 PM GMT, on April 12th of 2066, every communications satellite, television set, and computer on Earth had been bombarded with... everything. The signal had been strong enough to blot out every form of communication on the planet, and had lasted exactly six minutes.

Within days, world governments had convened a series of special meetings, and within weeks the signal had been traced here. To this otherwise unremarkable piece of interstellar space.

All the world's instruments were trained on this spot and the scientific community was baffled to find this, a completely stationary asteroid, alone in space billions of miles away from anything else. It shouldn't exist, it couldn't exist.

And yet it did.

What's more, the signal remained. It no longer drowned out the Earth but it shone, a steady beacon to those who were listening.

The Source galvanized mankind, revealing to all the world that the issues which had for so long divided them were petty, trivial compared to the knowledge that something was out there. Work was done in decades that would have taken individual nations centuries to accomplish, progress and innovation flourished as never before.

All leading to this moment.

"Miranda, do you read us?"

She blinked, her eyes dry, unsure just how long she'd been standing, staring off into space.

"Sorry, yes, I read you, control."

"Thank God, we thought something had gone wrong," the voice said, clearly relieved. "What happened? We lost all comms with you."

"The signal flood projecting from the entrance is too powerful for my suit, it overloaded everything, please advise."

Silence.

"Control?"

"Standby, Captain."

God how she hated that phrase.

Miranda waited as patiently as she could as seconds turned to minutes.

"Captain?"

"Yes, control, I'm here."

"Captain, this is Admiral Colin Reeves, UPN Commander."

Miranda's cheeks flushed with embarrassment at her flippant response, this was one of the most important men in the world, he'd designed most of the equipment she wore.

"Y-Yes sir!"

"I'm talking to you now not as a superior officer, but as a fellow human being. We don't know how this ends, we don't know what happens in that hole. No one can rightly ask you to go down there, knowing you'll be totally isolated. We can pull you back, consider other options. No one would fault you for-"

"I'm good, sir."

She surprised even herself. She hoped her voice was steady and cleared her throat to speak again.

"Sir, I'm ready. I'm here. I'll do it."

"Then Godspeed Captain, we're all behind you."

Miranda heard a faint beeping and noted mentally that her heart rate was in the yellow, 130 beats per minute. She silenced the alert and closed her eyes, focusing solely on her breathing. After a few moments, she opened her eyes again and stepped to the very edge of the entrance.

She hammered one last stake into the ground, clipped on her tether, and then leaned forward over the opening.

With her mag boots on max, she could walk down the edge of the tunnel with relative ease, so she took a tentative step down into the unknown. She held tight to her tether with one hand as she made her way down the tunnel. She felt the familiar tug of gravity as she approached the light below. That wasn't possible either, this tiny asteroid should have had such a negligible gravity field that she shouldn't have felt a thing.

She grew closer, and it grew stronger.

As she approached, she could see a thin membrane, like the surface of a massive bubble, was the source of the light and, theoretically, the signals. She could see herself reflected in the shimmering surface as she got closer.

She looked at her HUD, everything was still normal. No temperature spikes, no unusual radiation, just the mass of communications signals and the strong gravimetric anomaly.

She was a foot away now, maybe less, and the gravity was strong enough that she felt as though she were suspended from the sky, hanging out over the pool of light and mystery.

A moment of fear passed through her heart, chilling her briefly.

But how could she give up now?

She took a breath, closed her eyes, and fell forward into the unknown.

3

The God Of Particles - Robert Owen

Ramon Garciaparra paused at the door to check the nameplate; the sign proclaimed Security Office Large Circular Collider MIT. He felt some of today's irritation wash away with the realization that the flatfoot's directions had got him through the subterranean warren after all. A strong scent of tobacco emanated from the room beyond.

Pushing through the door into the campus security nexus he was almost overwhelmed by the fugue of cheap cigarette smoke within. Waving the nicotine fog from his watering eyes, Garciaparra made out two occupants in the windowless den.

Leaning back on a desk opposite the door was a smart looking guy with greying hair, holding a lit cigarette poised over the lip of a disposable cup. Between drags, dead ash dropped unnoticed onto his tailored suit, his attention otherwise focused on the bank of television monitors arrayed in the corner

In front of the CCTV screens perched the second occupant, a mousy looking man in a drab lab coat, the long fingers of one hand drumming out a frantic tattoo on the worktop whilst the other hand pivoted back and fore on a large dial like a safe cracker searching for the magic combination.

"You know it's against Massachusetts state law to smoke in a workplace? Even a world-famous workplace." Garciaparra's announcement of his presence startled both men, the suit dropping his tab into the plastic receptacle, and the lab coat jerking the dial violently, eliciting a frustrated snarl.

"Christ! Jesus, man, if you saw what we have, you'd be sparking up too."

"Twenty years since I last toked, so I doubt it. Heard you guys were looking for me."

The suit glanced at the badge hanging around Garciaparra's neck and offered his hand as he stepped away from the desk, "Thanks for coming down here Detective…"

"Garciaparra. Cambridge PD." As he took the proffered hand, the detective sized its owner up further, ex forces he concluded to himself, not the easily rattled kind.

"Duffy Lewis, Chief of Security for the project. Guess we solved the mystery of our missing scientist…if we can verify the security footage is real."

"I thought the feed for last night was corrupted. Unrecoverable, the patrolmen told me upstairs."

"Unrecoverable, unless you're a genius like Glen here, he was able to reconstruct the night's take from a hard drive back up." Lewis indicated the other LCC employee as he spoke.

The lab coat named Glen gave a ghost of a smile, eyes darting around the room, "I prefer stable genius, Mr. Lewis, labelling someone as just a genius makes it sound like they're crazy."

"A hard drive? I didn't think they even made those anymore." Decades old tech in the world's most advanced lab piled on the weirdness of this case for Garciaparra.

"With all the particles whizzing around down here, they have triple redundancy on most systems." Lewis shrugged, "a lot of expensive equipment is all I can say."

"Well, what have you got to show me? There isn't a lot else to go on right now." Garciaparra flipped out his notebook and skimmed his notes, "Dr. Adeyemi arrives for work on Tuesday morning and hasn't been seen since. Car is still in the faculty lot, no signs of a struggle inside, bank account and credit apps untouched. Husband called in a missing person's report on Wednesday morning."

"Well...Glen was checking the date stamps to make sure what we were looking at was...real." The Chief of Security's eyes unfocused for a moment and he swept his hand through his trimmed hair as he spoke.

"You think you may have been hacked?"

"Not possible with the hard drive. Remotely anyway. It's not connected to any external infrastructure."

The lab coat piped up, "I've concluded that whatever we saw, it wasn't AI generated or even good old CGI."

"Lord, it's real?" Lewis's voice faltered, and he slumped back onto the edge of the desk, producing a polished cigarette case from inside his jacket.

"Well, I guess real is subjective, Mr. Lewis," Glen pushed his glasses back up his nose as he spoke, reminding Garciaparra of Clark Kent, "but is this feed a fake? No. Whatever that was, the camera recorded it faithfully."

"Look guys, this has not been a fruitful day so far, so if this footage means I can get home on time, let's get on with it." The detective moved around behind Glen and stood facing the monitors. "I finally got tickets for the Green Monster seats tonight and I don't intend missing out, it's only the Expos, but hell I've been waiting two whole years."

Garciaparra heard the snap of a lighter closing behind him, as a fresh wave of tobacco rolled over, "I don't think you'll be too concerned with the Red Sox tickets Detective, once you've seen…the…footage. Roll it Glen."

The stutter in the Chief of Security's voice was matched by the screens as they blinked into life, painting a deluge of rectangular afterimages on the detective's retina.

Finally, the displays snapped into coordination and Dr. Adeyemi's office leapt into life, with each panel showing a different angle of the same frame.

Garciaparra had become acquainted with the room during the day and noted nothing was out of place from the current arrangement. The bookcases were stacked with journals as now, and the back wall was adorned with the same professional qualifications and accolades.

What was new was the sight of the eminent scientist in the flesh. Hmm, seems younger than her official photos, the detective made a mental note to update his pad once the viewing was done. With her pinned up hair, smart blouse, and prim glasses, Aisha Adeyemi was the epitome of a scientist type in Garciaparra's eyes. She was peering at a bulky folder of printouts, a folder that wasn't in the catalogued items of her office.

He frowned, his eyes struggling with the grainy footage, he turned to Lewis to ask why that was, but the chief was ahead of him.

"Yeah, I know. The data is compressed, to fit on the hard drive. Looks like an old VHS feed doesn't it?"

"I wouldn't know, does it?" The detective chuckled, "You're older than you look man."

Lewis smiled wanly in response, his hand shaking as he took a drag, "I'm going to sit back here while you watch, not sure I want to see it again right now. Or ever."

Garciaparra shrugged and returned his attention to the bank of monitors, he blinked.

Where the hell did he come from?

Standing in the middle of the room, a couple of paces from Dr. Adeyemi's desk was an odd-looking dude.

The guy was white, around five-eleven, and had a severely receding hairline, the remains of his greying hair was buzzcut, giving it a scruffy appearance matching the rumpled white shirt he sported. He wore his sleeves rolled up and the shirt collar open. Unlike most of Collider staff there was no tie, instead a large lanyard was draped around his neck ending in a chunky looking photocard.

As Garciaparra squinted to read the undecipherable symbols on the photocard, he gave a start as Dr. Adeyemi did the same on screen, sitting bolt upright in her chair.

"Who the bloody hell are you? Who let you in?" The doctor wasn't expecting her visitor.

"I let myself in. Quite easily. Is your data interesting?" The unknown man pointed at Dr. Adeyemi's work, his accent was cut glass British, like a villain in an action movie.

"Well that's none of your business, now I'm giving you thirty seconds to leave on your own accord before I call security and they throw you out on your bony looking arse."

The man smiled, or rather, sneered at the doctor, "Oh now, now. I don't think you want me to leave, you want me to stay and have a little chat. A little chat about those results you've got there."

Dr. Adeyemi's body stiffened for a microsecond, followed by a vigorous shake of her head. She looked at her guest as if trying to place his face before smiling at him.

"Please, won't you take a seat, Mister...?" Adeyemi proffered the man a chair with a stiff hand gesture.

The man sneered.

"I have many names. Today, you may call me...Loki."

The monitors crackled. The man was sitting in the chair immediately in front of the doctor.

"Your results, Doctor Adeyemi." The man known as Loki flicked a bony finger towards the data folder on the desk.

"Oh yes, yes of course." She beamed at the man, her voice racing. "Well not so much interesting, as quite well astounding!"

"Do tell."

"Well almost unbelievably, this contradicts all the data we've collected globally on the Higgs-Boson particle for the last two decades. If this isn't a massive system error, then almost everything we thought we knew about the Standard Model and the universe is wrong." Childlike excitement radiated from the face of the eminent physicist.

"Yes, I thought you might come to that conclusion. Why were you looking at the God Particle anyway, I thought you were investigating other issues during this period."

Adeyemi pulled herself up in her chair and tutted like a school ma'am, "Now, we don't use such loose terminology as that. That misnomer is inaccurate, the product of sensationalist journalism in the nineteen nighties. Higgs himself would be turning in his grave."

"Again, Doctor, what were you doing looking at the God Particle?" The voice was icy.

The physicist giggled, "Don't call it that!"

"You would be surprised how accurate that misnomer is. Now, again, why?"

"So, we accelerate two different streams of subatomic particles to ridiculously high levels of kinetic energy and then we mash them together! Like two cars playing chicken, but badly. The Higgs-Boson particles fly off like burning car wheels."

"I know all this! Why, doctor? Why? My patience is tiring." If the voice was cold before it was now down at absolute zero.

The doctor's face formed into a childlike pout, "We weren't. So there. We were investigating the state of the early universe via Quark-Gluon Plasma. The data suggested an anomalous reading on Higgs-Boson decay, so I went and checked. Clever me."

"Yes, clever you, unfortunately." The man called Loki sighed and leaned back in his chair, "you see, Doctor, this is the problem with breaking in new…interns, shall we say. They tend to slack off when they should be concentrating. Have you ever had that problem?"

"Oh yes, some of them were really dumb, I mean really, really dumb." She giggled again and unpinned her hair with a lazy finger.

"None of you here in this circular collider of yours, or that decrepit version in Heidiland, were meant to see how the God Particle really works." He shook his head ruefully, "We can't have that getting out, my…colleagues and I have invested a lot of work in hiding the true nature of your environment from you."

"Our environment? You mean universe, silly." The giggle this time was halting. Forced.

"No, I mean your environment." Loki paused and rubbed his chin, "I'd like more of your normal self back for this next part."

The monitors crackled as one.

The doctor sat bolt upright in her chair, her hair ragged, a sheen of perspiration visible on her forehead.

"Don't be ridiculous, that whole life is a simulation rubbish is passé, the product of the same juvenile minds that thought parallel worlds meant somewhere else you were Beyoncé."

"You are right of course, this is not a simulation, more of a controlled environment." His lips arced upwards, but the eyes were flinty.

"Like a zoo then, and you, you are our god? Gods?" She laughed but her voice was strained.

"So close that I will not disagree with you." The humourless smile was unmoving.

"Tell me then, oh God, why do you make this world so awful, eh? The death? The unnecessary suffering? The conflict? What kind of gods would do that to their followers?"

"Ahh, a small correction after all then. Not a zoo, more like a farm."

"What?" Adeyemi's voice rose in pitch, and her breathing picked up pace.

"Yes, a farm. My kind have fed on your kind since you first gained sentience."

"No. No. No... I refuse to believe that we are living in an old Keanu Reeves film, this can't be right." The doctor's breathing was rapid, she swung her head around the room.

"True, we don't use you for energy, and you didn't create us. No, we use you for sustenance."

The doctor gave an involuntary yelp.

"We have roamed the realities since time immemorial looking for lesser species to feast upon. Once we hunted you one at a time, and you called us Daemons. To be honest though, I found that time consuming and inefficient, so I persuaded my brethren to adopt more modern practices."

"We're...your...cattle?" Hyperventilation forced the doctor's words out haphazardly.

"More like poultry, you're free range after all." Loki cackled and now there was real emotion behind the gaze.

"But how can you feed on us? When we die our bodies are interred, or cremated. I don't believe you!" The physicist's denial was loud but hollow sounding.

"Oh, we don't feed on your flesh, nothing so barbaric. Nothing so primitive, no, we feed on your consciousness, your soul as you like to call it."

Adeyemi shook her head, words failing to leave the petrified mouth.

"You asked me how we could be so cruel earlier? Well, frankly, because it makes you taste better. All the suffering makes you...juicier." He licked his lips as he spoke, as if relishing a delectable morsel.

"Evil...Evil. Demon."

"Demon? Yes, OK if you want. Evil? No. Practical." Loki stopped to wipe a modicum of drool from the corner of his mouth, "I mean you do the same. You fatten your own livestock; you eat their young. You tenderise meat by hammering it, you marinate food with hot spices to cure them."

He shrugged. "So, you see, I can't let this data leave the room. I mean, imagine the mess it would make if your chickens started to revolt."

From somewhere, Doctor Adeyemi found a burst of adrenaline and kicked herself away from the desk, falling backwards in her chair.

Bouncing to her feet, she burst for the door. As she cleared the desk, Loki stretched out a long leg, impossibly long, and sent the physicist tumbling to the floor.

As the doctor tried to untangle her legs, Loki rose from his seat and stood over her.

"You know some of us still like to hunt you on occasion, for the sport they tell me. I didn't understand why they bothered...until now. I'd forgotten how...visceral this feels!"

Loki's body exploded outward, a mass of darkness, a hint of black leathery wings here, a glimpse of thrashing tentacles there. The writhing blackness engulfed the office, blocking the CCTV capture of Dr. Adeyemi almost completely, her patent leather shoes the only remaining sight of her existence.

The feet could be seen scrambling backward, the sound of hysterical sobbing proof that the physicist could still be heard at least. A glint of something hard and shiny shaped like a talon rose and then fell swiftly. The sound of something wet and soft tearing.

The screaming began.

Twenty seconds later the kicking feet stopped, and the screams ended. The screens cut out.

Garciaparra raced for the waste bin he'd seen in the corner, when he retched, he realised someone had used it for the same purpose earlier. As he heaved his afternoon coffee and donuts into the trash receptacle, he felt a hand on his back.

"I know man, I know." Lewis was shaking himself as he did his best to comfort the detective.

Through gulping breaths, Garciaparra managed to speak, "That's not right, it's not possible."

"I know, I know." Repeated the security chief.

"No, I mean it's not possible. The crime scene team swept the office looking for a sign of struggle, there was nothing, nothing out of the ordinary. Not even under UV, just some minor stains like any old office." The detective straightened as he spoke, using the bare concrete block wall for support.

"That's because, unlike my incompetent intern, I am very thorough. I'm not likely to miss a localised backup for example." The British accent cut the air like a shard of jagged ice.

"Jesus!" Garciaparra and Lewis whirled to face the new voice.

Glen had gone, his murky lab coat shredded on the floor, in his place sat a figure familiar from the CCTV playback.

"No, not quite." The thing sometimes known as Loki responded, rising from the workstation as it did so.

It dominated the middle of the room, even in its human form, though Garciaparra could now see how that label wasn't accurate. The skin was sallow and looked leathery like old paper, yet somehow crisscrossed with fine cracks like an old china cup.

"You may call me Loki, or Nyarlathotep, or any of a thousand other names. Not that one though."

The tobacco fog was blown away by a foul stench as it spoke, reeking of formaldehyde and the worst viscera Garciaparra had witnessed on the autopsy table or in the morgue.

Covering his mouth with one hand the detective reached for his piece with the other.

"Ah yes, I have one thing to be thankful to my intern for. At least I'm finally getting out and getting some exercise."

The room went dark.

The sound of a firearm discharging echoed in the corridor outside, followed by the sound of screaming and inside, flesh tearing.

After two minutes there was only silence.

4

Reinventing the Wheel
- Liz Shipton

"It's not ketamine." Lugh shook the dime-sized baggie of white powder between two fingers and held it up to the light. "It's time."

Morrigan felt her face become an incredulous maze. "Time? What the fuck do you mean, it's time?"

"Time. You know, time." Lugh flicked the bag. "Moments. Centuries. Eons. The wisest counselor of all. The thing that waits for no man." He tilted an eyebrow over the bag at Morrigan. "Or woman."

"I know what time is, asshole. What I'm failing to comprehend is how you somehow found a fucking bag of it."

Lugh shrugged. "I know a guy."

Morrigan folded her arms with an impatient sigh as he peeled open the tiny Ziploc. He sniffed it carefully. He closed one eye and squinted into the top. He raised his eyes back up to Morrigan's.

"You wanna try it?"

"Do I want to try snorting time?" Morrigan didn't unfold her arms. "Well, gee, I guess I'm all done smoking space so sure, why not?"

Lugh jangled his keys from the front pocket of his pants, dipped one into the bag, and pulled it out with a tiny white pyramid of powder on its tip.

He hesitated. "I mean, worst case scenario, it's actually just ketamine, right?"

"Worst case scenario?" said Morrigan. "No, worst case scenario, it's actually fucking time and we get totally fucked. What is it even supposed to do?"

"To be honest, I have no idea." He lifted the key and carefully held it out to her.

"You want me to go first?"

"You always go first."

Morrigan watched him, chewing her cheek. "If this is powdered sugar again and I'm sneezing white boogers for a week, I'm going to be really pissed."

"It's not."

His face was serious enough that Morrigan unfolded her arms. "Alright," she sighed, perching on the edge of the bed, "lay it on me, Doctor Strange."

Lugh knelt and touched the tip of the key below her nostril and Morrigan plugged the other side of her nose and sniffed hard.

It was as though she had fallen face-first into the sea. As though someone had put a water gun full of battery acid up her nose and pulled the trigger. Morrigan tried to gasp, but before she could do it, her mind went loose around the edges and the meniscus of her consciousness overflowed its brim. The chasmic, star-studded cosmos rose up around her and she sank backward into inky oblivion.

When she came to, she was standing in a field.

"Fuck me," she gasped, as every breath she had ever taken evacuated her lungs at once. "Jesus." She doubled over with her hands on her knees and stood there, panting, until she felt the prickle of eyes on the back of her neck, and bolted upright and spun around.

Behind her was a man dressed in a grubby tunic and layers of shawls, with shabby leather sandals strapped around his feet and an impressive thicket of hair sprouting from his face. He was half-crouched with one arm raised, a stone-headed hammer clutched in his fist, and was glaring as warily at Morrigan as she was at him.

Morrigan lifted a hand. "Hey there."

The man tightened his grip around the hammer and said nothing.

"Sorry for the uh—I'm, uh, not here to ruin your day or anything." She glanced around. The man was standing in front of a round hut made of animal hides stretched over a wooden frame, behind which was a small semi-circle of similar huts. To the man's left was some kind of workbench strewn with tools. Tall grass and trees stretched as far as Morrigan could see. In the distance, a herd of something that looked like bison were shifting like a dark cloud across the plain. "Where are we?"

The man stared at her like she had appeared out of thin air. Which Morrigan supposed was fair because, as far as she could tell, that was exactly what she had done. She lifted her hands as though placating a wild animal and tried for a pleasant smile.

"It seems like you maybe don't speak my language. I don't want to spook you, but I have no idea where I am…or…potentially, when…so I'm wondering if maybe you can help me figure it out."

Gripping his hammer, the man watched Morrigan slowly approach until she was close enough that she could have grabbed the weapon from him if she was fast enough. Instead, she slowly lowered both hands, and as she did, the man lowered the hammer. Morrigan tapped her chest. "Morrigan."

The man nodded.

Morrigan refreshed her smile and peered around his shoulder at the workbench. It looked as though he had been in the middle of something when she arrived—a stone chisel lay in the middle of the bench next to a pile of curled wood shavings. Next to that was a wooden disc, about three inches thick and a foot and a half in diameter, which had apparently been hewn by hand with the chisel. It looked like some kind of giant wooden coin, and had been carved with astonishing precision. Morrigan frowned. This was either the weirdest K-Hole she had ever been in, or Lugh's bag of time had actually opened up some kind of wormhole and sucked her into the past.

The man's gaze followed hers to the wooden disc. To Morrigan's surprise, he grinned, held up one finger, then ran around to the other side of the workbench and hefted the thing into his arms. He tottered backward with it and set it down, balanced on its narrow edge. He nudged it with his toe and it rolled a few feet and then toppled over, like a coin on a table. He grinned up at Morrigan and raised his eyebrows, as though he had just performed an incredible magic trick.

"I don't know what you want from me, man," said Morrigan.

Sighing, the man shook his head and righted the disc. He rolled it back to the workbench and leaned it up against the corner, then scratched his chin and stood there contemplating it.

Finally, Morrigan said, "Hold on…is it…a wheel? Are you trying to make a wheel?" The man frowned at her.

"A wheel." Morrigan came around to his side of the workbench and contemplated the wheel. "I think for that you need a—what do you call it? The bit that goes through the middle. An axle!" She snapped her fingers. "Check it out."

She knelt and traced a small circle at the center of the wooden disc with her finger. "You need to cut a hole here. Then put something through it; a stick or something." She cast about and spotted a long stick on the ground. She picked it up and placed the tip of it against the center of the disc so the man could see where to put the axle through. "See what I mean? Then you can attach stuff to the axle and make, like, a cart and use it to carry stuff around. It's way more complicated than that in practice, I think, but...you seem pretty skilled. You can probably figure it out."

She squinted up at the man, who had one hand on his chin and was frowning at her. By degrees, as she watched, the light of understanding came into his eyes. His face cleared. He snapped his fingers and pointed at her.

Morrigan nodded. "You get it?"

~~~

When Morrigan emerged from the inky black soup of the cosmos and returned to her bedroom, Lugh was waiting. She rolled over, gasping, and sat on the edge of her bed with her forearms on her knees.

"How was it?" said Lugh.

"Fucking crazy."

"It worked?"

"I think so. I think I invented the wheel."

Lugh was very quiet for a long minute. Then he said, "You did what?"

"The wheel! I think I invented the wheel. Well, actually, technically, I guess I invented the axle. The guy already had a wheel." Morrigan grinned up at him. "Man, that was—" She stopped. Lugh's face had paled.

"You invented the wheel?" he said again. He was still holding his keys and the little baggie of white powder, and now flung them aside and lunged for the door. "God dammit!"
~~~

"What?" Morrigan stumbled after him.

Lugh was halfway down the hallway outside, a cavernous marble tunnel with gilded pillars and arched doorways yawning on either side of it. "Dagda is going to fucking kill us!"

He was running flat-out and Morrigan lost him around the next corner. When she finally caught up to him, he was at the Viewing Window with his palms flat to the glass, staring down at the Earth.

"This version wasn't supposed to have the wheel!" he panted, as Morrigan pulled up next to him. "It was explicitly stated in the charter document."

"Why not?"

"Because the wheel is the beginning! It's the root of all the problems. The wheel means mechanization of agriculture. Transport! Economy. The wheel makes capitalism possible. Capitalism! You wanna deal with fucking capitalism again? You remember what a nightmare that was?"

"I don't understand—"

"Why do you think we had to apocalypse the last version? If we hadn't sent that plague, they'd still be down there on their fucking smartphones, drinking almond milk and arguing about gun control. Dagda spent, like, ten thousand years repairing the mess they made. And this version was going along fine!" He turned to the window again. "We made it all the way to twenty twenty-four. Now look."

Morrigan turned her face to the window. The Earth, which just ten minutes ago had been a beautiful blue-green marble spinning gently around the string that tethered it to the firmament, had changed. Gashes of black and brown covered the bit where the Amazon had been. Most of the United States was on fire.

"Shit," whispered Morrigan.

"Yeah. Not super great, Mor." Lugh dragged one hand down his face. "Dagda is gonna be so pissed when he finds out we have to apocalypse these guys again."

"Well for fuck's sake, Lugh!" she cried. "If that time shit was so risky, why did you even give it to me? Where did you even get it?"

Lugh grimaced. "I don't know. Some Norse guy."

"Some Norse guy? Some Norse guy like who?"

"That guy who's always hanging out with Onuava."

"Loki?!" Morrigan's voice rose an almost perfect octave. "You bought drugs from Loki? What were you thinking?"

"He made it sound like no big deal."

"Well, I'm not going to be the one to tell Dagda his project is getting apocalypsed again. I'm not the one who bought fucking drugs from fucking Loki, the Trickster God."

"Yeah, okay—" Lugh shut his eyes. "Fine. You're right. I'll tell him." He heaved a sigh and turned back to the window. Morrigan did the same, and they stood with their foreheads pressed to it in silence, watching the ice caps melt.

"Twenty twenty-four," said Lugh quietly. "I guess it's further than we got last time."

"Do you think they invented the internet this time around?" Morrigan asked.

"They always invent the fucking internet, Mor."

5

Molars - Saylore Doom

We are a civilization that has existed for millennia, stretching our existence across the vast and immeasurable expanses of the cosmos. Time, as you understand it, has little meaning to us. We have outlived the rise and fall of stars, witnessed the birth and death of galaxies, and watched as the universe itself has expanded and evolved. We were not always as we are now. Once, long ago, we were bound by the limitations of physical form, tethered to a single world, experiencing the universe through the narrow scope of our five senses. But that was an age so distant that it has faded into myth, lost in the vast repository of our collective memory.

We shed those primitive forms, transcending the constraints of flesh and bone to become beings of pure energy. In this new state, we were liberated, freed from the burdens of physical existence. We no longer needed to eat or sleep, no longer felt the sting of pain or the weariness of age. Our consciousnesses merged, forming a vast, interconnected network of thought and knowledge, an eternal, collective mind. In this state, we roamed the stars, gathering knowledge, exploring the mysteries of the cosmos, and contemplating the deeper truths of existence.

We have no need for bodies, for we are not bound by the physical laws that govern the universe. We have become something greater, something more profound. We exist as pure energy, capable of traversing the vast distances of space in an instant, of experiencing the entirety of the universe in ways that those still bound to flesh could never comprehend. We have reached a level of understanding and enlightenment that transcends the limitations of the physical realm.

And yet, as the eons passed, we began to realize that something was missing. Despite all our knowledge, despite all we had achieved, there was a void within us that we could not fill. We had forgotten the simple pleasures of existence, the joy of sensation, and the richness of experience that comes from living in a physical body. We had forgotten what it meant to feel, to truly feel, in the way that only those bound to flesh can.

The memories of our corporeal past had faded into obscurity, becoming nothing more than abstract concepts cataloged in our vast database. Words like "warmth," "cold," "softness," and "pain" were mere entries, devoid of meaning or context. We could recall the definitions of these words, but we could no longer grasp their essence, their reality. The sensations they described were beyond our reach, lost to us forever in our state of pure energy.

It was then that we realized the depth of our loss. In our quest for enlightenment, we had left behind a part of ourselves that we could never regain—not through knowledge, not through exploration, not through contemplation. We had lost the ability to feel, to experience the world in the way that we once had. And so, we began to yearn for something we could no longer remember, something that had been so integral to our existence, yet had slipped through our fingers like sand.

This yearning grew within us, a longing for the sensations and experiences we had forsaken. We desired to reclaim the ability to touch, to taste, to see the world through eyes of flesh. But our energy forms were incapable of such things. We were beings of pure thought, existing in a state of perfect understanding, yet we could no longer experience the simple, visceral pleasures of life.

And so, we began a project, one that would take millennia to complete. We set out to create new bodies, vessels that could house our essence once again. But these bodies would not be the frail, imperfect forms we once inhabited. No, they would be designed with the precision of eons of knowledge, crafted with the full understanding of the intricacies of life, death, and evolution.

We started with the most fundamental building blocks of life—DNA. We meticulously designed the genetic code that would guide the development of these new forms, ensuring that they would evolve and adapt over time, becoming more perfect with each passing generation. We did not rush this process, for we knew that true perfection could only be achieved through the slow, steady march of evolution.

The first iterations of these new bodies were simple, almost primitive, by our standards. They were living organisms, capable of basic functions, but far from the perfection we sought. Yet, even in their simplicity, they held the potential for growth, for improvement. We watched as they evolved, generation after generation, each one building upon the successes and failures of the last.

We crafted neural networks with the utmost care, designing them to mimic the intricate pathways of thought and consciousness. These networks were not mere circuits of metal and wire, but living, organic systems, capable of carrying the electric impulses that would give rise to thought, emotion, and awareness. We knew that these bodies would need to be capable of experiencing the full range of sensations that we had lost, and so we designed them to be sensitive to the world around them, to feel pleasure and pain, warmth and cold, comfort and discomfort.

As these bodies evolved, they began to take on more complex forms. They developed limbs to manipulate their environment, eyes to see, ears to hear, and tongues to taste. They grew in intelligence, becoming more aware of their surroundings, more capable of interacting with the world. Then they began to form societies, to create cultures, to build civilizations. They started to explore the mysteries of their own existence, seeking to understand the world around them, just as we had once done.

Yet, even as they progressed, they remained unaware of their true purpose. They believed themselves to be the masters of their own destiny, the pinnacle of evolution, never suspecting that they were merely the latest iteration in a much longer process—a process that had been set in motion long before they ever existed.

We watched as they built great cities, as they developed technology and art, as they made war and peace, as they sought to conquer the stars themselves. Their achievements were impressive, but they were still far from the perfection we sought. They were still evolving, still growing, still learning. We waited patiently, knowing that the time would come when they would be ready—when their bodies would have reached the point of perfection, capable of housing our essence once again.

Over countless generations, we observed the subtle changes that marked their evolution. We had encoded a marker deep within their DNA, a sign that would indicate when they had reached the desired stage of their development. This marker was a vestigial trait, a remnant of their primitive past—molars, the last vestiges of a time when their ancestors needed to chew tough plant matter to survive. As they evolved, this trait began to disappear, generation by generation, until finally, it was no longer present in their genetic code.

The absence of molars in the last generation was the signal we had been waiting for. It marked the completion of our millennia-long project, the culmination of our efforts. Their bodies were now ready, perfected through countless generations of evolution, capable of hosting our consciousnesses once more. The time of our return was at hand.

Yet, they remained blissfully unaware of their true purpose. They believed themselves to be on the brink of a new era, poised to explore the stars and unlock the secrets of the universe. They had no idea that they were about to fulfill the destiny for which they had been created. They did not realize that their creators were waiting in the wings, ready to merge with the bodies they had so carefully crafted.

As the final child was born without molars, we prepared for our return. The harvest of flesh was at hand. We would descend upon our creations, merging with their bodies, reclaiming the sensations and experiences we had lost so long ago. We would once again walk among the living, feeling the warmth of the sun on our skin, the taste of food on our tongues, the joy of laughter in our hearts.

But as we prepared for this moment, we knew that there would be those among them who would begin to understand the truth—those who would see through the veil of their existence and realize their place in the grand design. They would see the signs, the patterns that had been woven into the fabric of their reality, and they would know that they were not the masters of their fate, but the creations of a civilization far older and more advanced than they could ever comprehend.

That's why we send this message to them, to reward them. If you have read this far, the truth should now be clear. You are not the pinnacle of evolution, but a step in a much longer journey. You are not the creators, but the created—designed and perfected over millennia to serve as vessels for a civilization that transcends the limits of flesh and bone.

You are destined to contribute to our great civilization, to become part of something far greater than yourselves. You are our creations, and we are coming for you. The time of our return is near, and soon, you will fulfill the purpose for which you were designed. Prepare yourselves, for the harvest of flesh is at hand.

6

Three's Company - LeAnne Keely

"How long's it been Zeke?"

Zeke looked over, his scratched, dented motorcycle helmet hiding his facial features behind a black, mirrored visor.

"Hmm?"

Ariel sighed, the vapor turning to steam as it left the ports of the gas mask she wore.

"Nevermind."

Zeke shrugged, his trademark hodgepodge of hockey pads and body armor rustling over his broad, muscular frame.

Ariel checked the charge on her motorbike. It was low, only 30% if her gauges were to be believed. But then, that's what they were doing here after all. She gently pressed the accelerator with her booted foot. The bike whirred to life and rumbled down the crowded streets of Old Chicago.

They passed the burnt out hulks of thousands of cars. The crumbled ruins of skyscrapers that must have been beautiful in their day. Of course, the distinction between Old Chicago and New hardly mattered, they were both wastelands now. World War Five had seen to that, or was it Six? After a time it got hard to tell them apart, but back when they were still receiving broadcasts from the Capital in California there had been plenty of experts to debate whether Five had ever really stopped.

She shook her head to clear the ashes of her memories and ran a hand through the thin, wispy remains of her hair. The radiation therapy pills were working, but only to delay the inevitable. She'd been blonde when she was younger, now her hair was the same gray as everyone else's.

Even the corpses had gray hair.

A soft beep drew her attention back to her battery readout, it was down to 25% now. The damn thing had been holding less and less of a charge lately. She almost never rode it this low, but resources were scarce. Now more than ever.

They wove in and out of traffic, doing their best to avoid the newer cars. Those nuclear batteries were notorious, and the more time went by, the more likely they were to crack, explode, or leak. No point in upping your dosage. As they rode, she paused periodically to check her compass. Most of the time it pointed North, naturally, but they were great for sniffing out live electromagnetic charging stations in the city.

Ah, speak of the devil.

She glanced at the instrument, either she'd gotten herself very turned around, or it was now pointing due West. She gave a short whistle, easily heard over the soft hum of the bikes.

Zeke turned in her direction, but was characteristically silent.

It took some searching, the stations tended to polarize any surrounding metal, but eventually they traced the source of the magnetic field to an underground parking garage. The door was shut, but it didn't present much of a challenge.

Zeke made a habit of carrying a high powered laser for just such occasions. Using it was a risk, not only because any mistake with it was potentially lethal, but because they had to slave it to one of the batteries if they wanted to power it. Endangering the batteries was tantamount to playing Russian Roulette, no one survived without transportation out here.

They'd learned that many times over.

Zeke popped off his bike, the suspension almost sighing in relief as he dismounted. Ariel had an equally important job, keeping watch. She unholstered the shotgun she kept in front of her left thigh. It was a Marvis Arms 860, developed sometime in the mid 2300's, but even being an older firearm it was highly reliable. Its most useful feature was easily the method by which it fired. It magnetically charged, then repelled a ferrous slug at insane velocities. Whether by design or oversight, it had the ability to fire any iron-based object that would fit in the barrel. This quirk of engineering made it absurdly versatile since The Fall, and she'd seen men killed over the mere suspicion of possessing such a weapon.

She had a few real shells, but chose to load it with ball bearings or bits of rebar for the most part. Anything under 3 ounces would still break the sound barrier.

She watched from the street, knowing that her companion would alert her to anything below. The high-pitched whine of the laser started down below, and she could smell vaporized metal. Sharp, acrid smoke wafted up for a few minutes while Zeke worked, but he was done in short order.

Silence from below told her he was ready.

She took one last glance around, then drove her bike down the ramp to meet him. She caught his eye, and took a glance at the rifle on his back. He must have agreed, because he adjusted his sling so that the weapon was on his chest.

They rode together into the unlit confines of the parking garage. Their approach must have set off a motion sensor, because bright halogen lights flickered on above them, revealing a dozen charging bays. Three of the bays were occupied by vehicles, the rest lay empty. What looked like an elevator shaft sat at the back, presumably it led to the building above and had been used by the workers there.

A quick search of the room revealed nothing untoward. In fact, judging by the several inches of dust on everything, this bay had remained sealed since the battlefront had moved north to the Soviet lines in former Canada decades ago.

Ariel parked her cycle and ran diagnostics on the bays. The first several were useless. They had power, but the coils were off. She'd gotten an explanation once from a man who called himself a physicist. He'd told her, way back when, that magnets under pressure like these required calibration so that their polarity didn't "undergo radical shifts, misaligning the entire machine."

He was a nice guy.

He hadn't lasted long.

She sighed wistfully, side-eyeing her friend. It was a wonder they'd lasted so long. Then again, they lived by strict rules. Rules that had been learned the hard way, and which had proven themselves over and over.

She was relieved to find that the sixth and ninth bays both worked, so they'd be able to charge both cycles at once. All the better. Her cycle was at 11% by the time she got it plugged in. She thought about mentioning it to Zeke, but decided not to. No reason to worry him, he already fretted about her enough. In his own way.

With their power needs met, she turned to their next task, food.

Zeke was ahead of her, he'd already unpacked their small stove and was boiling water from a jug. There wasn't anything to be done about the rads, but at least they could avoid bacteria. Most of the strains that had survived the wars were chemically resistant, but sometimes the best solutions are the simplest. Boiling still killed just about anything.

The tiny device was bubbling away nicely within a few minutes, meanwhile he rummaged around in the saddle bags of his bike. She watched him as he carefully retrieved a protein paste ration tube and unsealed one end of it. He pulled the brownish rod from within the tube and retrieved a knife from his belt. He precisely measured two servings, about an inch of paste, and cut it off. Not a single crumb was wasted, it all either went back into the tube, or into the pot of boiling water.

She allowed herself to relax a little as she watched him. His studious, carefully calculated movements always put her at ease. It was one of the ways that she knew he cared. His every action was an economy of movement, a conscious decision of when and how to spend energy. She admired him for it, how could she not? His senses were also excellently tuned, a fact that had saved them many nights before.

She was unsurprised then that he heard their visitor before she did.

He cocked his head to the side, freezing as he stirred their simmering dinner.

Arial stood, turning to the entrance as she shouldered her shotgun. Zeke slipped behind one of the parked cars, hidden from view of the entrance, his large body as silent as a shadow.

"I come in peace," the stranger called out, freezing just inside the doorway they'd cut in the plasteel of the garage door.

He had his hands up at his sides, but the man wore pistols at his hip.

"Are you alone?"

He nodded, not taken aback by her greeting or her question.

"I am, and you?"

"Perhaps," she replied vaguely. "You a walker?"

He smiled.

"Ain't no walkers anymore, parked my bike outside."

He nodded at the bays.

"You mind? I need a charge ma'self."

She considered it, then nodded.

"Set your guns down, then you can bring her inside."

He seemed to weigh his options, but in the end he slowly and deliberately removed his gun belt. He laid it gently on the ground, then slid it out of easy reach with his foot.

"Good?"

She nodded.

"Let's go get your bike."

"You mind givin' me a hand," he looked embarrassed. "I ran out of juice a few blocks back. Been pushin'."

She allowed herself a smile, it happened to everyone eventually. Took a tough bastard to survive such an event. Or a lucky one.

"Thought you said you wasn't a walker."

"Yeah, yeah," he shrugged.

She followed him outside at a distance, making sure he went first.

Her jaw dropped a little at the sight of his vehicle. It was a Sclera Valkyrie, not a jury-rigged rat-rod like the ones she and Zeke were riding but a real, factory bike. Matte black and slate gray curves put the rusty bolt-bucket she drove to shame, and it looked extremely well cared for. The machine was heavily laden with supplies too, a full half dozen saddlebags, and it even pulled a small, make-shift trailer made of scavenged parts with a tarp over top.

"No wonder your batteries died, hauling all this."

He shrugged.

"Well, you see anything you like, maybe we can work out a trade."

She took another long look around, there were no signs that he'd been lying about being alone either.

"Alright, stranger-"

"Jeremiah. Name's Jeremiah."

She started over.

"Alright, Jeremiah, you grab the front, I'll push from back here."

"Doesn't seem right," he said. "You gettin' the heavy end."

"Chivalry's dead, Jeremiah."

He couldn't argue with that, so he simply shrugged and grabbed the handlebars of his bike, pushing it towards the entrance to the garage. It took them several minutes before they got the machine down to the door, and they were both breathing hard and sweaty.

"Almost there now, Jeremiah, don't give up on me yet."

He wiped his brow.

"Ya know usually you tell someone your name they tell ya theirs back."

She looked into his eyes, surprised at the genuine softness she saw there.

"Sorry Jeremiah, rule six."

"Rule six?"

She nodded, leaning into the bike once more.

He followed suit, but wouldn't drop the subject.

"Ah, so what, rule six means you don't share your name with anybody?"

"Something like that, yeah."

They cleared the doorway of the parking garage and found themselves once more within the well-lit confines of the bays.

A single shot rang out as Ariel crossed the threshold, and she flinched as Jeremiah's head exploded into a spray of brain and bone fragments. He slumped to the ground, his body not even twitching as it lay there.

She sighed again.

"Sorry to keep you waiting, Zeke," she called out.

He walked over beside her and put an arm around her shoulders.

"Rule six," she mumbled, shaking her head.

Zeke nodded.

"Three's company."

She looked up, surprised he'd spoken aloud, but he was already searching through the saddlebags of their new vehicle.

"How long's it been Zeke?"

Zeke didn't answer, he rarely did.

7

First Contact with the Enemy - June M. Burton

"This is JMS Madrigal, go ahead Vaudeville. Over." Petty Officer Warren barked into the com. The bridge was silent as the void.

"Madrigal, this is Vaudeville. We are taking heavy fire from an Imperial dropship. They have a fist of Armor on the field and are pounding us with their main particle cannon." Warren blanched at that and looked around at Commander Kolchek and Captain Judith, who commanded the two hands of powered armor based on the madrigal. Judith grimaced and made a hand signal to Lieutenant 'Dogmeat' Figueroa. The commander nodded his ascent. The two paladins strode off the bridge without a single word.

"Crew to level one combat readiness, and tell Chief Technical Officer Ginnestera to get the Vikings rearmed and ready for action. Ensign Toshima set course for the Vaudeville's last ping. Let's go save our sister!" Commander Kolchek squawked in his nasal voice. The bridge exploded into activity as the crew jumped to begin preparing for combat.

"Sounds like your ass is really in the fire, Vaudeville. The interdiction squad is en route to you, and we will be there to provide fire support in short order." Petty Officer Warren nearly shouted over the fresh commotion. The reply was lost in the din of screaming alarms and running feet.

Deep in the bowels of the ship Captain Judith was joined by the rest of the paladins that made up the heavyweight hand that gave the Madrigal its vaunted status in the Jesuit fleet. Judith was giving them a run down on the situation as they headed for the Armor bay. She finished her briefing and asked for questions. Ensign Harris, fresh from the seminary, put up her hand. Judith nodded in her direction.

"Captain Judith, I'm sorry, but which Armor am I assigned to for this mission?" Her voice shook a bit. She knew the fearsome reputation of the Madrigal's interdiction force but she hadn't ever sortied with them.

"Grab whatever machine you're most comfortable with. You haven't been here long enough to have one modified for you yet." Judith replied with a smile at the young pilot.

"I trained on a Bashi-Bazouk in seminary. Is that Viking with the two autocannons available?" Harris asked.

"That was Lieutenant Rupar's. Feel free to take it." Judith said. What went unsaid was that Rupar was dead, shot down 2 weeks before. That's why Harris was there, all shiny and new.

"They had a compensatory setup for the left gun on account of the range of motion problems they had with their left shoulder after they lost that arm. It's pretty easy to figure out though." Dogmeat added cheerfully, they had been close with Lieutenant Rupar, and the two had flown each other's machines in training exercises.

"They had hardware?" Harris asked, sounding shocked. During her training she heard that prosthetics were the end of most pilot's careers. The slowed reflexes caused by the mag connectors hardware utilized were untenable in combat situations. Dogmeat laughed and rolled up a pant leg to show the composite trestle and synth muscle that replaced their leg below the knee.

"You spend enough time with us, you might end up with your own. We're all hardwired though, none of that mag lag." Dogmeat rolled their pants back down.

"You're not."

"Damned right they are. It's old school, but it works." Captain Judith said as the group neared the airlock.

"It's barbaric! The surgery alone ought to be a crime. Let alone how much time it takes off your life." Harris spluttered. Dogmeat clapped her on the back.

"We're all living sortie to sortie here. If I make it back alive, I thank God; if I don't, I meet the Devil."

"Enough. Stop scaring people, Dogmeat." Judith said absently as she searched the bustling armor bay for the chief armor tech. "Just keep your head on straight, and kill the enemy, Harris. I'll make sure you make it back alive."

"Yes Ma'am." Harris said.

"Ah, here's Alfredo!" Judith said, her hawkish face cracking in a smile as she spied the heavyset Armor tech. The pair hailed each other and Judith called out. "Is the interdiction squad rearmed and ready?"

"Yes ma'am! You're ready for combat." Chief Technical Officer Ginnestera said, snapping off a crisp salute with his mechanical right hand.

"Good. Ensign Harris will be flying the Viking with the extra auto cannon."

"We thought she might be, so we got it rearmed for her. Do you know about the compensator, Ensign?" Ginnestera asked.

"Lieutenant. Figueroa let me know." Harris replied.

"Alright folks, let's get suited up and get under way. Every minute we waste here is worth five on the battlefield." Judith said. No one argued.

Inside of five minutes, the entire squad had donned their blue and white environmental suits, and were headed for their armor. As they made it to the lifts, the ship's chaplain intercepted them. With no preamble he launched into a blessing.

"So I say to those of you who are present, hear me. Know that you are the striking, vengeful hammer of God. Sally forth, and save your brothers in arms, no matter the cost, for God shall forgive any trespasses, and grant you absolution. In the name of the Father, the Son, and the Holy Spirit."

The young man rattled off with all due reverence. The paladins bowed their heads, and murmured amen as one at the finish. The chaplain accompanied them up the lift to the scaffold that ran behind the armor. As each paladin swung into their cockpit, the chaplain made the sign of the cross and said softly "Go with God."

~~~

Ensign Harris saw the flashes of light in the distance almost as soon as they launched. The armor had all been equipped with drop tanks of extra fuel that would allow them to reach the battlefield without taping their primary tanks, and they plunged through the void at a breakneck pace for armor the size and weight of what they were flying. Two Vikings held the flanks of the formation, with a captured Dragoon backing one, and a Hussar backing the other. In the lead was Captain Judith's battlescarred Crusader. All five machines had been freshly painted in Jesuit blue and white, but each still showed the repair patches Chief Technical Officer Ginnestera's techs had welded in. Ensign Harris thought that the squad looked more like a bunch of ragtag pirates gone a-raiding than the crack strike force of paladins she had been told she was joining. She found herself watching Captain Judith. The giant Crusader had about two meters on even the Dragoon, and it was heavier and wider. The shape was more like a man in a suit of plate and mail than the more simian form of the other heavy armor.
~~~

When she had seen Crusaders flown at seminary they were clunky and slow, but Judith seemed to dance around the asteroid field that separated them from the edge of the battlefield.

"Alright folks, drop tanks here and engage armor at will. I need you to keep them off my back. I intend to sink this goddamn ship before it sinks the Vaudeville. Fall back to the debris field if you suffer damage." Captain Judith's voice came over the com.

Ensign Harris took a deep breath and hit the switch to drop her external propellant tanks. The Viking instantly became easier to maneuver and she dodged below a chunk of burnt out hull, and streaked towards a pair of red and gold Imperial Hoplites that seemed to be providing overwatch for the enemy. Harris drew a bead with the right autocannon, but the left one was far too sensitive moving left to right so she squeezed off a single burst from the right. The depleted uranium screamed across the void, and slammed into the egg shaped armor, cracking heavy plating but not penetrating. Harris dodged left as the Hoplites swarmed towards her like angry bees, auto cannons ringing out shot after shot. The Viking had maneuverability against the lighter Armor, but she had far more firepower to bring to bear.

She sent another burst from her right autocannon at the Hoplite closing from her left and she almost squealed with delight as it ripped the autocannon array off the side of the little Armor. Without so much as a breath, she swung the Viking around and took a shot at the other one with the left gun. Dogmeat was right, it was easy to get the hang of. This burst slammed the thick frontal armor and deflected, and as the Hoplite entered melee range, it unleashed with its light laser, slagging the shroud of the right gun. The egg-shaped armor pirouetted as it climbed, tempting her to follow. Instead she dove for the other one. It still had its gun.

Some primal part of her training kicked in and as she dove, Harris flicked out the tungsten rod that lay in the forearm of all Viking derived Armor and it heated to screaming, white-hot plasma. Suddenly an alarm blared through the cockpit. She ignored it as she closed on the Hoplite and drove the rod through the chest of the enemy, and ripped it to the side, putting the Hoplite well out of the fight.

She swooped and made a full force climb back towards her other opponent. She was closing, she could taste the fiery end of the other Hoplite if only that incessant alarm would shut up! What the hell was it?

She broke off her ascent and brought the left cannon to bear and sent a spray of uranium rocketing into the Hoplite which broke for home as its armor plating was ripped free. Harris couldn't resist a parting shot which slammed into the thruster cluster mounted to the back and stranded the little Armor. Finally, she powered down the plasma blade and checked her instruments.

She found that the alarm was an overheat warning, though now that the tungsten was cooling, she could see that she had slagged her own gun barrel with that stunt. Harris jettisoned the useless weapon and sighed. That left her with the twitchy left gun at range and the plasma blade in close. No sweat, she'd been training for this for 6 years.

Judith streaked across the battlefield, moving the heavy-weight Armor as if it were a natural extension of her body. It came so easy now, it was a heady feeling being one with a machine that could take down any other Armor ever built in one- on- one combat. She searched the panoramic view and spied a trio of Dragoons heading for the edge of the battlefield. Ensign Harris was the only one in that area. Damnit all, she needed to sink this drop ship but she couldn't leave a rookie pilot facing three missile boats. With a sigh, Judith broke off her pursuit of the ship and focused instead on the three sharks scenting blood in the water. She was quickly in gun range at the expense of propellant. The enemy were moving slowly, probably conserving fuel given how long the battle had been going on. Judith opened with a charged particle salvo from the torso mounted cannons, then belted the closest Dragoon with a burst from the Crusader's heavy autocannon.

The sizzling purple globes of charged particles flew wide of their marks but scattered the formation, and the splintering armor of the last Dragoon bore witness to the awesome power of the autocannon. She had to be cautious with the ammunition however, for she had only enough shells for 10 seconds of continuous fire. The Dragoon with the damaged armor spun to confront her, unleashing a flight of light missiles and unsheathing a tungsten plasma blade, gripped in its right manipulator. Judith unleashed a cloud of Vulcan cannon fire from the shoulders of the crusader, knocking out a few of the missiles. She threw up her shield and promptly lost roughly a quarter of it as one missile slammed home, but the last two didn't track her heat signature and flew wide. The Dragoon started a full throttle charge towards Judith's Crusader, blade couched like a knight's lance. She began a climb, banking hard to the right and kept her eyes on the Dragoon as it followed her.

Suddenly it broke off the pursuit as the right arm was detached in a hail of autocannon fire. Judith scanned the area and caught sight of a Jesuit Armor at the edge of visual range. In a moment, the targeting computer identified it as Ensign Harris's Viking. The disarmed Dragoon was breaking for home now, and Judith let it go, searching for the enemies she knew were out there, waiting for their opening.

"Nice shootin' Tex." Judith said, keying her com.

"Thank you ma'am." Harris replied.

"Thank me when we land, Ensign," Judith said. "For now let's fall back to the debris field. Even with you backing me up, two Dragoons at once is a tall order. We engage at close range and move from cover to cover to avoid missiles."

"Yes ma'am. Moving out." The Ensign rattled off and made for the debris field at high speed. Judith was impressed, most paladins fresh from seminary would have struggled to adapt to a customized machine that wasn't theirs, let alone perform such maneuvers as Judith could follow on the ion trail.

"The girl has promise as long as she doesn't get her fool self killed," Judith whispered to herself, or maybe to the Crusader, it was hard to tell which was which when she was slotted. Her physcom scores were through the roof and the neurolink slot at the base of her skull allowed her the kind of control of her armor that an unmodified human being could only dream of. The tradeoff was anti-rejection drugs, regular courses of antibiotics, and a potent antipsychotic to keep her mind whole when she became one with her machine.

The priests told her it was a gift from God, but Judith never set much store in divine blessings, preferring to trust in an extra ton of armor and the heavy autocannon. She shook her head and cleared her thoughts. Those Dragoons were still here somewhere. She accelerated into the debris field and started the hunt.

Judith followed the tell-tale ion trail of verniers and caught sight of Ensign Harris tucked up beside a piece of a downed ship's hull. The Viking looked rough. She'd had to jettison the main gun and had her plasma blade extended but not burning. Judith keyed her com.

"Keep moving, Ensign."

"Yes ma—" the Ensign's reply was cut off by an alarm sounding. A fusion pulse had been detected at 5 o'clock high, and Judith spun to defend without a second thought. A flight of short range missiles blazed across the inky void, and an answering volley sprang from the Crusader's autocannon. Judith opened up with the shoulder Vulcans again but it was too late. Of the six missiles, three found their marks. Judith got her shield up in time and took two of them, trading the huge plank of Ferro-fibrous composite to save her body armor. In the split second between her autocannon volley slamming home and the Dragoon closing to melee range with Harris, Judith swung the left manipulator in an arc and landed a crashing blow to the opposing armor's cockpit then drew back and flicked out the tungsten core of the mighty plasma blade.

Ensign Harris was in trouble. The debris wasn't enough to fox the Dragoon's salvo and a missile slammed into the center of the Viking's torso, stripping armor and damaging the hydraulics. The left arm ceased to traverse horizontally. Harris didn't think, there was no time to. She kicked her right pedal and spun the armor to face the Dragoon bearing down on her with a plasma blade in hand. It was inside the minimum effective range for her autocannon but she put a volley into the enemy regardless. The rounds stripped armor from the shoulder and Harris ignited her own plasma blade and made a clumsy parry of the enemy's starbright sword. The missile strike had crippled the right arm as well, making it sluggish moving up and down, so she hit the throttle and rocketed away from the Dragoon. The heavier armor made to follow, but Ensign Harris lost it quickly, and a blinding flash from behind her told her that Captain Judith had finished the enemy off—or vice versa. No time to think about that now, she needed to get clear of the field and return to the Madrigal before she became salvage. She broke for home, and heard the alarm as a fusion pulse closed in.

The Dragoon was an ugly devil of a machine. Heavy simian limbs sprouted from a bulky body armored to hell and back. They were designed as short range brawlers, aiming to get in close enough to unleash hell from four 6 missile pods then go to work with a pair of plasma blades.

It appeared on the rear monitor like a great charging red bull, chasing her with long horns of white hot tungsten extended. Harris spun her machine, flying backwards, avoiding a meteoroid narrowly before she got a clean line of sight. Aiming was out the window with the hydraulics in the shape they were in so she pressed the trigger and unleashed a five second burst as the Dragoon closed, hoping to catch the enemy in the hail of gunfire. She was thrilled to see chunks of red and gold armor flying free of the other machine. She ignited her own plasma blade and locked the arm in place, then pulled up hard and launched the Viking at the Dragoon. The pair closed in a flash and the blades clashed with a wave of heat like a desert summer.

Then, they were passing each other.

Harris dodged the hulk of another heavy Armor, long since destroyed, then circled back searching the void for the Dragoon. She spotted it and started her swoop, unlocking the arm at the last minute and letting it sag as she adjusted the flight path of her armor to pass above the enemy. Another wave of heat filled the cockpit as the three blades clashed again. This time there was a loud groan from the tungsten and the Viking somersaulted away as the Dragoon reversed course and swung the blades in wide arcs as it closed again. Harris lost the right leg of the Viking before she could stop the spin. She feathered the verniers to correct, then swung the burning blade across the body in a feeble attempt to riposte. She hit the throttle and pulled away from the Dragoon as warnings flashed and claxons screamed in the cockpit. The leg was gone and the whole Armor was crabbing badly without the leg mounted verniers. The hydraulics were toast, and the armor was in real danger of going into fallback mode, shutting down weapons and redirecting power to the life support systems. She thought about punching out, but she couldn't guarantee that she wouldn't be immediately taken prisoner. Instead she locked the arm at right angles then braced for impact, and most likely death. She hit the throttle, running balls to the wall, and whispered to herself,

"Hail Mary, full of grace, for the Lord our God is with you—"

~~~

Harris woke in the med bay of the Madrigal. Lieutenant Figueroa sat in a chair to the right side of the bed, snoozing with their head on their chest, legs crossed so Harris could just see the prosthetic leg as the hem of their pants pulled up. Her head was full of bees, buzzing pleasantly, but her left arm was in agony below the elbow. She came to a horrible realization as the pain settled in. The arm might not be there anymore. She looked straight up, afraid of what she would, or wouldn't, see when she looked down. The memories of the battle swam through the sea of bees. The last clashes with the Dragoon came to the fore then sank away as she came to that final charge. Harris had been sure she was going to die, but here she was.

Figueroa started from their nap.

"Holy shit, you're awake?" The Lieutenant blurted. Harris tried to answer but it felt like her mouth was full of marbles.

"Yes, Lieutenant," She rasped eventually, in a voice rusty with blood.
~~~

"Oh hell, the doc said you'd be out for another day at least. Lemme get him." Figueroa rose and stepped out of the room. Harris kept her eyes to the ceiling, willing her brain to stop buzzing and bubbling. Before long Lieutenant Figueroa was back, accompanied by Captain Judith and a tall man in white that must be the doctor.

"Well Harris, you made it back alive." Judith said, walking to the bedside.

"Yes, Captain." Harris said, throat starting to loosen.

"You've been promoted for your actions in helping to save the Vaudeville. Three and a half kills, including a Dragoon in single combat, is quite the feather in your cap, Lieutenant Junior Grade."

"I shot down the Dragoon?" The memory washed over her as she said it.

The Dragoon barreled towards her, blades held wide. As she prayed to the virgin she accelerated and the gap closed in an instant. The enemy's plasma weapons snapped shut in slow motion as her own went deep into the chest, carving downwards as she sought the reactor. She was going to die but she was taking this bastard with her. The blades slammed into the Viking's arms and carved them off. It was too late though, the damage was already done. The reactor went critical and the explosion tore the damaged Viking to shreds. The last thing she remembered was her arm shredded by the glass that exploded from the left monitor, and the warning that her life support system had been damaged.

"You also scored a half kill on the one in the debris field and forced the other from the field." Judith's voice brought her back to the present. "You're one and a half kills south of being an ace."

"We recovered your gun camera footage." Lieutenant Figueroa burst in. "That stunt you pulled fighting those Hoplites was incredible, and the way you took out that last Dragoon was almost poetic. Ginnestera is pissed at you for tearing up his baby though. He loved that Viking."

"Thanks, and thanks for letting me know." Harris said, not knowing what else to say. The rust was falling off her voice now though. It was time. She finally looked down. She wanted to scream but it caught in her throat. She looked up and saw the doctor step forward.

"I think that's about enough for right now." He said, addressing the pair of officers, trying to shoo them from the room. "Lieutenant Harris and I have a serious conversation to attend to."

"One last thing, Doctor," Judith said as the door slid open.

"Absolutely not, Captain. Please leave." The doctor said, interposing himself between Harris and Judith. Judith clenched her jaw and shook the doctor's hand, then walked out, Lieutenant Figueroa on her heels. The doctor shook his head as he shut the door. He sat down in the chair and looked hard at Harris.

"I won't sugar coat things Lieutenant, the glass shredded almost all the flesh on that arm, and you'd lost so much blood by the time Captain Judith recovered you, we had to take it. That's not all. You've also got six broken ribs, and two fractures to your skull. The most important part is the arm though. It needs surgery and it needs it soon, before bone callus forms and we have to cut away more. We have sourced a mag link system from the Vaudeville's medbay and we can operate tonight. It'll mean relearning how to use that arm, and you won't be flying Armor again, but you'll have—"

"No." Harris said, guts churning. She was one and a half kills from being an ace in one sortie with the interdiction squad. Besides that, Harris had never felt as afraid or as alive as she had on that battlefield. That's what she had trained for six years. She wasn't about to be a chair jockey. She knew what she had to do.

"This isn't me asking, Lieutenant, this is me telling you what's going to happen."

"No it isn't," Harris spit and waved the bandage swathed stump of her arm at him, "because you're gonna hardwire me."

8

Breathe - Jan Abel

The office of Dr. Reinhard Schreiber was located on the fourteenth floor of the Taylor Building in uptown Lansing. The building itself was filled with various shops and offices, ranging from a prom dress store to an energy drink start-up

Marbled floors echoed my footsteps as I came to a stop in front of the door. A wooden bench sat to the door's right, and a privacy screen had been put on the glass of the door. In a dark, golden font, I was greeted by the words "Office of Dr. R. Schreiber, Psy.D., MD."

Just as I raised my hand to knock, the door swung open and I came face-to-face with just who I had come to see.

Schreiber was a balding man with thin lips, and his olive-toned face was clean shaven. He wore a tan sweater vest with a white collar peeking out from the top as a suede suit jacket covered the rest of his chest. He was a striking figure compared to the bland halls, but his smile was kind as he stepped aside to motion me in.

"Miss Ryan, I'm glad you could make it this afternoon."

His accent was thick with his original German, but after a year of seeing the man, I had come to honestly find a bit of comfort in it as I tried my best to give the man a small smile and step over the threshold.

"Thanks for fitting me in, Dr. Schreiber," I said quietly, not meeting his eye as he shut the door behind me. "Sorry for the last-minute ask."

"It is not a problem," he assured me as we made our way to the usual seats. "I was growing concerned for you after your third cancellation this month," he admitted in his blunt way.

I ducked my head and tried to not look him in the eye. I really had meant to make it to the last two appointments, but every time I had tried to leave my house, I just couldn't bear the thought of even getting out of bed.

Taking a breath, I tried to relax into that familiar half of the couch.

In, 2, 3, 4; hold, 2, 3, 4; out, 2, 3, 4.

Dr. Schreiber had done a lot to differentiate his office from the clean—if a bit sterile—blues and whites and marbles of the Taylor hallway. The overhead lights were almost always turned off, replaced by some well-placed lamps and the two large windows at my back. He had covered the office in mahogany finishes, from the floor to ceiling bookshelves to my left, to the baseboards and crown molding, to his absolutely massive desk to the right of the door. I had never really seen him seated at his desk, the man usually always meeting me at the door and then sitting opposite of me in a wing chair next to the bookshelves.

In, 2, 3, 4; hold, 2, 3, 4; out, 2, 3, 4.

When I finally looked up at Schreiber, I found him patiently watching me, his notebook already in his lap, and a fountain pen in his left hand. Gulping, I gave him a small nod, an indication that I was okay, even if the term felt relative.

"I saw the obituary in the papers," Schreiber said. "I offer my condolences to the loss of your mother."

I looked away when his eyes met mine, tears beginning to well up again. I desperately tried to swallow around the rock in my throat. I had been hearing similar things for four weeks now, but it still didn't feel right. My voice was hoarse, as I thanked him, far too used to the call and response that came with condolences.

"Is it safe to assume that is why we have not been meeting at our usual times?" Schreiber asked, his voice level as he spoke, showing no indication that he saw my eyes tearing up again or the way that my upper body began to shake with the effort of keeping another sob at bay.

"I saw her that day," I whispered, knowing he would hear me. "I had gone over to help her put up her fall decorations. I had hugged her and said I would see her soon. I...I said I'd see her soon." There was no stopping the tears from streaming anymore and I collapsed down on myself, saying something I had already said multiple times in the last few weeks.

With my arms wrapped around myself, I saw through my swimming vision as Schreiber placed a box of tissues on the coffee table between us before leaning back, not saying anything as I hiccuped through another sob.

The office was quiet save for my cries and the soft tap tap tap of the metronome at Schreiber's side. I had been so out of it, I must not have noticed him turning it on. It took a few tries as I pulled myself together, trying my damnedest to match my breathing to the beats of the metronome.

In, 2, 3, 4; hold, 2, 3, 4; out, 2, 3, 4.

I'm not sure how long it took for Schreiber to break the silence, but it wasn't until my face was mostly wiped away. I knew I had been smart to go in with no makeup on, even if I may have looked like walking death as I came through the door.

"And they don't know who did it, correct?" Mutely, I shook my head, trying not to start crying again.

Murdered in cold blood, the officers had said. Seven stab wounds to the chest when she had been asleep on the couch, drunk. No fingerprints anywhere; no sign of forced entry. "How do you feel?"

A startled snort had me looking up at Schreiber.

"How do I feel about my mom being dead?" I asked incredulously.

"Yes, how do you feel about your abusive, no-contact, mother being murdered?"

"It was my mom," I asserted, voice rising, "how do you think I feel? We weren't always on the best of terms, but she was trying and she wasn't drinking as much and I had thought we'd have more time to work things out! But instead no, she got murdered in cold blood by some psycho and now she's dead, and I–"

"Breathe, Samantha."

In, 2, 3, 4; hold, 2, 3, 4; out, 2, 3, 4.

I cut myself off, gulping a few breaths. Schreiber broke the silence when my chest was no longer heaving.

"Nothing you have said today has been concrete about what emotions you are feeling," he said bluntly. We had spent three month's worth of sessions with him forcing me to learn how to catalog and sit with each emotion. I knew what he was getting at, even if he worded it like a dick. I sighed.

"I…I'm upset. I feel cheated. I feel abandoned like when I was little and she cared more about a deal at the supermarket than me. I…"

"You?"

"I feel relieved," I whispered, voicing what I hadn't put into words in four weeks. "And that makes me feel guilty. I'm relieved that I don't need to worry about her anymore or what she'll do to make my life hell, but then I feel like the world's shittiest daughter because who thinks like that?"

"Your feelings are complex because your situation was complex." He responded simply. "I was not aware you were in any contact with her to begin with."

"It was a newer thing," I explained quickly. "She had asked if I could help her get some boxes down from the attic because her hip was bothering her. She'd promised she would be sober…and, and she was! It was the first sober conversation we'd had in over a year."

I didn't explain how childish I was that day, how I'd felt like we could maybe have a chance at being normal. I didn't mention the hug she'd given me right before I left, and how I'd nearly had a breakdown then and there because how could this be the same woman that'd screamed at me over the phone a week earlier about stealing her booze and money when I hadn't been physically in front of her in months.

The metronome continued to click as Schreiber let me collect my thoughts, the gentle ticking nothing more than a background noise.

I had asked him once why he always had the thing going when we talked, or why his office was always filled with an incense-like haze.

A combination of ground Valerian, Kava-kava, and Passionflower, he had told me. Individually, and at a stronger level, the plants were apparently good sleep aids, and together could create a state of relaxation. It would help put his patients at ease when they entered, and they'd come to associate the smells with therapy and healing. He had also assured me that he wasn't affected by the scents as he'd lost his sense of smell years ago.

The metronome, he'd explained, was a constant force that gave his patients something to always center themselves with, apparently. One of the first lessons that he'd ever taught me when I'd begun seeing him was how to breathe with the metronome and balance myself when I was starting to get overwhelmed.

In, 2, 3, 4; hold, 2, 3, 4; out, 2, 3, 4.

"So what, it's like hypnosis?" I had jokingly asked him after a week of thinking about it. He had raised a singular eyebrow at me, his usual sign for me to continue my thought aloud. "I mean, think about it, all you're missing is the spiral or the pocket watch, but I've seen a couple of hypnotists at office parties. You've got the relaxing voice," I counted on my fingers, "you've got the ongoing smell, and the constant clicks. Face it, you're a closet hypnotist!" He had simply shaken his head at me, saying his multiple degrees made him a lot more than a party act.

"You said that the police have no evidence as to who it could have been?" He asked me after it was clear I didn't know what to say next.

I shook my head. "No murder weapon, no fingerprints, no evidence." Not even a doorbell camera for a clue. They had even taken to airing information on the local news on behalf of crime stoppers.

"What did you do with the knife?"

My head snapped up. "Excuse me?"

"The knife that stabbed her, what did you do with it?"

"Are you trying to tell me that you think I killed my own mom? That's fucking insane. I didn't kill her!"

"Do not lie to me, Samantha."

"I di–I, I–" Every single time that I went to argue, or just say 'I did not kill my own mother' it was like I choked on my own words. With dawning horror, as images flash banged my mind—blood on the carpet, the bottles getting knocked over, the blood arcing when the knife was ripped free, the screaming—I whispered "I killed her?"

All Schreiber did was nod, as if this were a thinking exercise, as if I'd just pinned down whatever emotion had been following me around like a cloud for a week.

Suddenly I was on my feet, making a beeline towards the door.

"I need to go. I need to go to the cops. I need to turn myself in. I killed–"

"Stop, Samantha."

My feet froze on the fancy carpet, my body lurching forward at the sudden stop. My hands were shaking and I felt like I was in a cage. I needed to get out of here. I needed to–

"Breathe, Samantha."

In, 2, 3, 4; hold, 2, 3, 4; out, 2, 3, 4.

"Again, Samantha."

In, 2, 3, 4; hold, 2, 3, 4; out, 2, 3, 4.

"Return to your seat, Samantha."

Never could I remember the doctor saying my name this often, as my body and mind were at odds and I found myself back in my spot on the couch, the cushions still warm.

"I will ask you this again," Schreiber said, his voice perfectly calm with a murderer separated from him by only a coffee table. "What did you do with the knife, Samantha?"

Black water roared below me. Flashing hazard lights of my car just behind me. Wind whipped my hair as I watched it fall, farther and farther.

"I threw it off of the Douglass Bridge near 37th Street. The gloves and the knife are both in the Grand River." I didn't recognize my own voice as I spoke.

Schreiber nodded. "Good," he said simply. "The current is fast enough that it will be long gone from the area by now. Any blood should be washed away as well. You did good, Samantha." Horrified, I felt proud under Schreiber's praise.

The pieces finally clicked.

"You knew I would do it, didn't you?" My voice was no louder than a whisper.

"I did. I'm the one who told you to do it."

"Why?"

Schreiber took me in for a second, almost measuring something, before beginning to speak again.

"Growing up, I did not have control of my surroundings. I, much like you, was at the whims of my parents. Going 'no contact' as it's popular today was a bit different before cell phones and instant communication. I moved to America for college and never looked back. I decided when I went into psychology that I would help my patients find that peace and freedom as well, whether it be through communication or action. In your case, action was necessary."

"You hypnotized me," I said breathlessly.

Schreiber gave me a singular nod, my eyes locked on his face.

"You can't do things you don't want to under hypnosis," I argued, whether with him or myself, I wasn't sure. "You can suggest things, but you can't force people to do your bidding under hypnosis, that's not how it works."

"That's not how cheap party tricks work, no," he agreed. "But multiple degrees based on understanding, directing, and reshaping the human mind is much more impressive than simply speaking to the subconscious."

"I'll go to the police," I avowed. "I'll tell them what you're doing."

"You will go to the police and admit to murder, but that you were hypnotized into doing it by your psychologist?" He said, his voice plain as he blinked at me. He spoke to me like a young child attempting to argue with a grown-up. "You'll be dismissed as hysterical at the death of your mother. You may be investigated, but you've hidden your evidence, and there's nothing to connect you to the murder of your mother besides your own word."

My horror only grew the longer Schreiber spoke, because he was right, I was backed into a corner. I had killed my own mother, and no one would believe that I had done it, or that he was involved.

My mom and I had never been each other's greatest support, and I had spent countless sessions on this very couch blaming her for how I was and what she did to hurt me. But she had been making a change, I was sure of it.

And now she never would.

And it was all my fault.

Tears silently streamed down my face as the metaphorical coffin seemed to seal me in. Schreiber watched me silently, his face impassive even as he closed his notebook and set his pen down on the side table next to the metronome. The damned thing continued to beat on at a steady tap tap tap throughout the room.

"While I understand your feelings now, this will be beneficial to you one day."

"Shut up," I grit my teeth. "Shut up, shut up. I'm going to live the rest of my life a murderer and you're telling me it's beneficial?"

"You will not live the rest of your life like this, Miss Ryan." I watched as he flicked one wrist looking down at his watch in a hauntingly familiar motion. "It would appear your session is nearly at an end. While I hate to leave any of my clients emotional, I'm afraid that will be how it will have to be this week." He waited until I met his eyes, and I felt as if I couldn't look away as he spoke next. "You will not remember this conversation, your confession, or your realization, Samantha. Feel how they pull away, dripping out of your mind at a steady drip, drip, drip."

His voice matched the speed of the metronome, even as I began to shake my head.

"Today," he continued in that same tone, "we discussed your feelings of sorrow and helplessness at the death of your mother, Samantha. But you eventually came to the decision that you will need to continue living, both for the memory of her you want to hold, and the younger version of yourself that had to survive growing up with her."

"I don't want this," I pleaded one last time, but even I could feel the way my body relaxed into the couch. I didn't want to forget what I did. I didn't want to forget that I had done something.

"This will become your reality when you've completed four deep breaths. You are safe here, as are your secrets," he reassured her. "Breathe, Samantha."

In, 2, 3, 4; hold, 2, 3, 4; out, 2, 3, 4.

Dr. Reinhard Schreiber had hypnotized me, making me murder my own mother. I wouldn't forget this. I was a murderer, and it was his fault.

"Again, Samantha."

In, 2, 3, 4; hold, 2, 3, 4; out, 2, 3, 4.

Dr. Schreiber used hypnosis in his sessions. I had murdered my own mother and told him about it. This was my fault.

"Again, Samantha."

In, 2, 3, 4; hold, 2, 3, 4; out, 2, 3, 4.

Schreiber used the smell of floral incense and the sound of the metronome in his sessions because they helped his patients relax during their sessions. I feel grief and helplessness for my mom, but I know I can always come to my psychologist. I'm safe here.

"Breathe for me, Samantha."

In, 2, 3, 4; hold, 2, 3, 4; out, 2, 3, 4.

My mom was gone, and I may never know what happened in her final moments. I need to keep going, I need to live on.

I sniffled, wiping my crusty eyes. I had known this session would be hard and I knew there would be tears but now I just felt exhausted, and my head was pounding. I took another tissue from Schreiber's box that he offered, cleaning off my face.

"I think we've made excellent progress today," Schreiber said as I collected myself, his pen and notebook now on his side table. The beat of the metronome matched the beat of my heart.

I nodded, crumbling the tissue and shoving it in my jeans as I stood up. Schreiber matched my movements, ushering me kindly towards his office door.

"Remember to give yourself grace, Miss Ryan. You are allowed to miss your mother–"

"–but live for myself, I know, I know," I interrupted him. From the sheer amount of times he'd said it in the session, it was permanently hammered into my head.

He offered me a small smile, dipping his head as I crossed the threshold back into the hallway.

"I will see you next week at your usual time then, yes?" When I gave him a halfhearted smile and nod, he dipped his head once more and the door to his office closed with a soft click.

Turning on my heel, I began the trek back to the elevator, my shoes beating on at a steady tap tap tap on the marble floors.

9

Mile Marker 98 - Siobhan Johnson

The primal scream ripped from her, scorching her throat and leaving her exhausted. It was a good exhausted however, the kind that helps you fall asleep for hours. And if she hadn't been driving, perhaps she would have shut her eyes for a while. Allowed dreams to capture her attention for a few hours, and take her away from this place. She still hadn't gotten used to anything really—beyond breathing the air. It was all foreign and uncomfortable.

As she approached mile marker 121, she swore and braced herself.

Light flashed and her head pounded from the force of the impact. The red Audi, that had been passing her, disappeared as did the semi-truck full of grain just three car lengths behind her. The seatbelt tightened, pushing the breath from her lungs, leaving them burning.

"Welcome back," came the disembodied voice. "Did you have a good trip?"

"Fuck!" was all Saoirse could manage, rubbing her chest and taking a deep inhalation of air. It felt good, familiar. The tang of carbon dioxide harsh on her tastebuds after having gotten used to the oxygen saturated environment of her 'vacation home'.

"You know it is more than a trip," she replied at last. "At least until you figure out how to prove my innocence."

"Ah, the conundrum," the voice replied.

"Conundrum?" Saoirse hissed. "This is more than a little problem."

"You were found 'holding the bag' as they say on that planet of yours."

"It is not my planet," came her reply through gritted teeth. "And I wouldn't have been holding anything if you and the others had done what you were supposed to do, when you were supposed to."

"I have told you more than once that we are not allowed to manipulate an individual into doing something they would not do themselves without our influence. So, clearly, he would never have done it himself."

The voice had a tinge of sarcasm to it that grated on her nerves.

"How do you ..." she began.

"Do you need a reminder of the events?" it asked.

Before Saoirse could respond, she was jerked into the past. She found herself standing next to Mathias, his body limp, gray and beginning to bloat. Turning away from it to retch, she was flung back to the moment before he had collapsed.

This time, however, she was seeing everything as a spectator; watching it unfold in front of her – unable to stop any of it.

"But Mathias, I can't just snap my fingers and provide you with a cure. That's not how this works!"

Saoirse saw her other self pacing back and forth in front of the man. He was slumped in a chair, hair disheveled, and a look of desperation on his flaccid face.

"I never should have come here. I should have believed you when you said I wasn't cut out for this planet," he muttered, barely audible to her sharp ears.

"Maybe that would have been best, but the fact remains, you did follow me here and now you... we're... stuck with the situation," she replied. "You had this illness on your planet. Did you think it would miraculously vanish when you arrived here?"

"Yes," he all but yelled back at her, suddenly coming alive. His face flushed and his breathing became labored. "You were going to be my savior! You were going to take me away from all of it! You were supposed to cure me, care for me, make me happy again!"

"Me?!" she repeated, flabbergasted at the audacity of his words. "How in the hell was I going to do all that for you? I am known for ..." she paused before taking a breath and continuing, "this planet is known for peace and balance. I don't have any powers beyond what you saw in those brief moments we shared in the beginning."

"But you tricked me. Admit it, you tricked me into following you here," he accused.

"I did no such thing," she growled back at him, feeling her temper rise.

As Saoirse watched, she recalled the anger she had felt during this exchange. Even now she could feel the disgust she'd had for the man she had once bedded. The scene playing out in front of her, her memory-scape, made her lips curl involuntarily with revulsion.

In a dizzy moment of vertigo, she was pulled forward. They were still in the same room, but the darkness outside the window told her they were close to the end of him. She had to admit she had knelt before her altar, many times, hoping for release from this human.

Wind whipped her hair across her face, and she realized the car window was down, and she was going much faster than the speed limit set by those who called themselves authorities on this stupid planet.

"Well, shit," she said as she applied the brake to slow the car. "Why can't I catch a break?"

Pulling off the road and stopping the car on the side of the off ramp at mile marker 123, she rested her head on the steering wheel and closed her eyes.

This had been happening more and more lately. She would find herself driving and approaching mile marker 121, when suddenly she was home, back on Venus, breathing the bitter-sweet CO_2 she missed whenever she took a breath here. The voice was asking her stupid questions and sending her back to that moment when he had finally died.

They'd sent her away when she'd been found next to his body. Back to his planet, to the time they had been together.

"Think about what you have done and return when you can accept balance and peace again," they had told her.

"I don't need to think about it!" she'd argued. "I didn't do anything. He did it to himself. Why can't you see that?"

"Beings from his planet are often weak, particularly the males. That does not mean that we can push them to their death …," they started to say when she interrupted.

"I did not do anything," she'd insisted. "He was particularly weak. He wanted me to cure him of all things! He wanted a miracle I couldn't give him. That's why he followed me here, that's why he's dead. Not because of anything I did!"

"Couldn't or wouldn't?"

Saoirse opened her eyes and flipped on her blinker to pull back on to the ramp and drive the remaining couple of miles to the house. She couldn't call it home, especially knowing that he was waiting there for her.

~~~

Mathias sat on the swing, staring at nothing in particular. She found him like this most days. His thermal cup would be filled with whiskey laced cola, a drink she could smell on him and which she detested. He'd ask how work was, and she'd make a noncommittal comment, that he wouldn't hear anyway.

She sucked in the oxygen laden air, trying to not cough at the lack of density it held. As usual, he invited her to sit
~~~

with him, although he didn't try to engage in conversation. It had been different once.

On her first visit to this planet, she'd found him and thought he was cute, in a lost puppy kind of way. They had mated a few times and, while she was underwhelmed, she returned to him on her second voyage. She knew the mistake was hers and had been unable to decipher what her lesson was supposed to be. Something she still found elusive.

As they sat in silence, she wondered what he would say if she told him about mile marker 121 and what happened most times she passed it. She was uncertain why she'd been able to make it back to this house some days without being transported home. She knew he wouldn't understand how the distance between it and the off ramp at mile marker 123 would be enough time for her to spend hours at home, reliving the events of October 28th. Not that he would know what that date meant to her, or himself for that matter, as it hadn't yet happened.

It's only two days away, she reminded herself. Can I change it? Can I stop this from happening?

In the relatively short time they had been joined, their living situation had deteriorated significantly. What had once been a more lively environment, had devolved into no conversations, bland fried food, and little to no physical contact. Not that she minded the last of those. She had found that just as on her home planet, she was better able to take care of her needs alone than with someone who did not want to focus anywhere but on themselves.

They moved through their evening routine of dinner, the idiot box (her not-so-uncommon nickname for the television set that took up most of one wall), and retiring to the bedroom at a ridiculously early hour, where he fell into a loud sleep while she picked up her latest book. Had they even kissed? She couldn't recall.

Letting the book drop to her lap, she turned her head to watch him. He lay on his back with his mouth agape, snores rattling from deep within his weak body. A feeling, akin to pity, churned her stomach.

If only I could see how he follows me, she thought, her book forgotten for a moment more. Perhaps if I distance myself from him? Maybe I should go to town and stay away from him. But how do I explain being gone for a couple of days?

Mathias rolled over, momentarily muffling his sleep sounds. The relative silence was broken, almost at once, by the shrill beeps of his alarm. Saoirse shut her eyes and waited to see if the sound would rouse him.

He rolled over and mumbled in his sleep. The alarm stopped. She knew it would begin again if he didn't take care of it.

As if on cue, the alarm sounded. This time she nudged him awake.

"What? Oh. Sorry," came his typical apology as he got up to quiet the alarm and check his blood sugar.

"You don't need to apologize, just take care of it," she replied.

Putting her book away, she rolled over in their bed and closed her eyes, hoping for sleep to descend quickly.

~~~

Waking up on the 27th, she was surprised to find him already up and drinking coffee on the patio.

"You're up early," she remarked, joining him by the fire pit.

"Yeah, couldn't sleep," he answered.

They sat in silence, watching the birds and squirrels enjoying the seeds he'd scattered for them.

"You seem … pensive," she said.

"Huh?"

"You seem to be thinking about something," she clarified for him, not sure if he understood the word 'pensive'.

"Hhmm," he paused, "I think I'll go to town with you today."

"Oh? Why?" she hadn't meant it to sound as harsh as it did. "I mean, what are you going to do while I am at work?"

"I thought I would go visit George. Then I could pick you up and bring you home. You said you only work half the day today, right?"

"Yes, I did. I just didn't realize you were listening when I said it," she joked halfheartedly.

"I do listen," he replied, an edge to his voice.

His alarm went off at that moment.

"Damnit," he began. "I fucking hate this goddamn disease. Why does everything have to happen to me? Why can't I catch a break?!"
~~~

His voice rose to a rant, a bitterness entering his tone, letting her know he was working himself into a rage. Internally, she cringed. They'd been over this many times and she'd told him she wasn't going to put up with it.

His emotional abuse was as old and pathetic as it was hurtful.

As he slammed his way into the house, she closed her eyes and sent another prayer to the Mother that she find a way out of this life, off of this planet—and soon.

Checking the time, she went inside and grabbed her purse and keys.

"It'll need to be another day," she began. "I need to get going and you're obviously not going anywhere for a little while."

"Like you give a fuck," was his retort.

"See you later," was all she said as she left the house.

Mathias waited for Saoirse to pull out of the driveway before he followed.

She's going someplace, and he'd bet it isn't to some job, he muttered to himself. Keeping a safe distance behind her, he trailed after in his truck.

Aware of the date, October 27th, Saoirse was on edge as she drove into town.

Will it be today? And how? Saoirse asked herself.

~~~

The nearby church bells rang in the noon hour as Saoirse prepared to leave her office. Her nerves ached from the stress. She felt the impending events deep within her. Dis-
~~~

tracted, she didn't notice Mathias in his truck until she was unlocking her car.

"What? You don't even say hello?" his harsh voice called out the truck window.

"Oh shit, you scared me, Mathias!" she squeaked. "What the hell?"

"I know you're hiding something from me. I want to know what it is," he hissed as she approached the window.

"I have no idea what you're talking about," she replied, attempting to keep her voice calm. She could tell he was in a worse mood than he'd been in when she'd left the house hours ago.

When he didn't answer, she turned and made her way to her own car, got in and started it up.

What do I do if I reach mile marker 121 and it happens again today? she asked herself.

Mathias followed her closely as she headed toward home.

She felt the vibrations by mile marker 98 and knew she was in trouble. So, this is how it happens. He just follows me across the line? How can it be that simple?

She tried calling Mathias on his cell phone and glanced in the rearview mirror to see if he would answer.

"What?" came his angry voice.

"I was just wondering why you are tailgating me?" she said through the car's speaker.

"I'm not. And what of it if I was?"

"I just don't want an accident," she replied, doing her best to sound calm.

Too late she realized mile marker 121 was next. The impact, again, knocked the breath from her.

Saoirse shook her head, feeling suddenly that something was different this time. Looking up, she saw that Mathias was lying a few paces behind her. She turned full circle to see if any of her sisters had materialized when they'd arrived on her home planet. Hearing a gasping noise, she quickly remembered that Mathias wouldn't be able to breathe easily here and ran over to him. Kneeling down, she breathed into his face, whispering the prayer, *breath of life and Mother, provide this man with the ability to draw in air as if it was his own.*

Gasping, Mathias struggled to sit up and breathe the carbon dioxide rich air.

"What... what, where am I?" he panted, staring at her in her true form.

Saoirse still knelt beside him, her short grey hair transformed to silver and her hazel eyes to a brilliant green.

"Mathias," she began. "I don't know how to explain this to you."

Sitting back on her heels, Saoirse closed her eyes and took a few long, deep breaths.

"Ok," she said at last, standing up and reaching out to take his hand. Pulling him to stand, she rolled her shoulders and smiled in what she hoped was a warm and welcoming way.

"Surprise," she said quietly. "Welcome to my home."

"Your home?" he said incredulously. "What the fuck do you mean by that? Where is my truck? Where is your car?"

"You need to tell him quickly, daughter, before everyone realizes he is here and descends upon you – and him," the voice said inside her head, speaking this way she was sure, so that he didn't hear.

"I will," she replied silently.

"Mathias, I don't belong to your planet," she began. "Remember, early on in our days together, I told you about Venus? We were laying on the chairs in the backyard and told you that story about being from Venus and pointed her out to you in the night sky? You laughed and asked me if, as an alien, I could cure your illness. When I said I couldn't, you told me you knew I was just joking. I let you think it. However, I wasn't—joking about being from another planet, not that I couldn't cure you. I meant that—I can't.

Well, somehow, and I don't know how, you have been pulled with me back to my home. You are on Venus."

"Yeah, right? What did you slip in my coffee this morning? What's going on? And if I am on Venus," he added, "how the hell can I breathe? Are you some kind of an alien after all or just trying to make me feel like an idiot?"

"Neither," she replied, trying to not feel insulted by his obvious prejudice. "I am a Venusian. And you can breathe because I prayed to Mother for you to have the ease of breathing our air."

"Gee how kind of you," came his sarcastic response.

"Would you rather I let you die?" she snapped before she could catch herself.

That is exactly why they think you kill him—tomorrow—thoughts and words such as those will do you no favors. The voice inside her head ridiculed her choice of words.

She watched Mathias as he processed the information she had given him. She could almost see the wheels turning in his head.

"So… this isn't Earth?" he asked. "So, things are different here?"

With a sigh, she acknowledged that yes, things were different here.

"HOW different?" he asked at the same time his alarm began beeping rapidly.

Before she could answer, Mathias let off a string of expletives and searched his pockets for his phone. Pulling it from his pants pocket, he jammed the buttons, trying to shut off the offending sound.

He looked up at Saoirse, phone in his hand, "So, can you do something about this?" he asked, holding out the phone.

"What do you mean?" she asked, knowing full well he was referring to his diabetes.

"I mean," he started, "can you do something about this and cure me?"

"No."

"What do you mean, no?" he said.

"Exactly what I said. No, I can't cure you here, anymore than I could cure you on Earth," she replied.

"Bullshit. I don't believe you," he shot back. "You can make it so I can breathe your air, why can't you get rid of this disease?"

"I don't have special powers, Mathias," she answered. "You can breathe here because I asked Mother to provide you with the ability to breathe, as if the air was your air."

"Then you can ask this Mother person to let me live as if I didn't have this disease," he argued.

"No, I can't."

"Can't or won't?" he asked, glaring at her with a venom she'd seen once or twice in their time together.

"This is your disease. I have told you that many times. I cannot do anything for you—you must decide how to live with it—or not," she said quietly.

"Live with it or NOT?" he sneered. "Oh, you'd like that, wouldn't you? If I just died."

"I said no such thing," she replied.

"Yeah, right," his voice dripping with self-pity. "If you can't help me, maybe someone else here can."

"Mathias, if there was a way for me or anyone else to help you, I would have told you," Saoirse told him.

"But you said you would help me. I remember it. When we took that trip to…where was it? You said you would…" he was weakening. "Why can't I see anyone else around here? How do I know this isn't some trick? Just send me home!" Mathias demanded.

"You mean when we went to the island?" she asked, momentarily confused. "I told you I would help you, help yourself."

"No!" The strength in his voice surprised her. "You made me follow you here; there must be a reason for it. You must be able to help me, and you just won't."

"I didn't make you do anything. You somehow managed to follow me across at mile marker 121. I don't know how to send you back. I don't even send myself back," she tried to explain.

Saoirse closed her eyes, centering herself, *I am at a loss here. Help me?* she asked, reaching out in thought to her sisters.

We cannot help you. This is your lesson, not ours.

And yet, you would ban me to Earth for his death? Just so I can learn some stupid lesson?

Opening her eyes again, she found their surroundings had changed. Mathias was now sitting in a chair—she recognized it with a plunge of her stomach. His skin was beginning to grey.

"Mathias?" she whispered, stretching out a hand to touch his arm.

His eyes were closed and his breathing shallow. Kneeling beside the chair, Saoirse felt for a pulse, finding it weak and thready.

You haven't much time left to reconcile this, to prove your innocence in his death, the voice told her.

"But you can see, I am not doing anything," she began.

"Precisely."

"What does that mean?" she asked, frustration evident in her tone.

"How can you resolve this situation? What can you see?"

"Nothing," she replied.

"Concentrate."

Resting her head on the arm of the chair, Saoirse closed her eyes and dipped into her memories, searching for a clue.

Images flashed past in rapid succession. Their trip to the island. His repeated questions about her past. The stories she relayed about her previous partners. His rantings about his previous partners and their lack of worth.

What am I looking for? The question asked more of herself than those joining her inside her own head.

"What lessons have you already learned?"

There it was.

As if flipping pages in a book, she went back to near the beginning of her intimate life.

From him, I learned that I am enough on my own.

From him, I found my voice.

From him, I was reminded to speak my truth and accept the consequences.

"And now?" the voice prompted me. "What have you found now?"

Mathias stirred, interrupting my thoughts.

"Hey," I whispered to him, "can you hear me?"

His mumbled response indicated an awareness of her presence.

"I cannot help you with this step, Mathias. You need to make this decision on your own," I spoke softly but firmly.

His alarm beeped again. The low alert made a familiar and unsettling noise, breaking the quiet of the room they were in.

For the first time since my awareness of the chamber, I looked around and found images, holograms of our brief life together. The early days when I had found him charming in a rustic way. The times I had saved his life. The moments when I had begun to question my sanity at staying. Red flashes of his rage, his ranting over the injustice of his life and all that had befallen him.

I could see it then, my lesson, glaring at me. It was so simple I was amazed I had not recognized it earlier.

"Yes? And what is it?" The question was quiet in my mind, asked by several voices blended together.

"I am only responsible for myself. I cannot make anyone do something they do not want to already do—whether positive or negative." I replied.

"At last!" the voices exclaimed, "And so?"

"Mathias," I whispered to his fading energy, "This is the path you have chosen. I cannot do anything to stop it. The strength or weakness is your own."

That I had thought my sisters and brothers here on my home planet could have—*or even should have*—done something was no longer important. I knew, now, that neither they nor I would have been able to change the path Mathias was on; we can only directly impact our own beings.

Before I could fully form another thought, I felt the pressure build and break over me as I returned to the highway. Off ramp 123 was just ahead of me and, as I watched, Mathias' truck flipped and rolled through the ditch off to my right. Slamming on my brakes, I pulled to the side of the road. Heart pounding and fingers fumbling, I punched in 9-1-1 on my phone as I pushed the car door open.

The truck came to rest on its back, wheels spinning and smoke billowing from the engine. I could see the roof crushed in on its occupant.

"Mathias!" I screamed, knowing at the same time that I wouldn't get an answer.

In the distance, I heard sirens. A semi-truck had pulled off the road ahead of me and two or three cars had come to a screeching halt not far behind. As we all stood there, watching, the truck exploded, shattered glass flying into the surrounding field.

I sank to my knees, understanding I had been returned to this place one last time so that his life could be resolved and I absolved of any wrongdoing.

10

The Mind Of Saumi Yanj - Laura Lee

1835 A.Y. Aush 6

Saumi Yanj was seven when she dissected her first rat, the blood pumping out from where she had sliced it open with an old kitchen knife to look at its still beating heart. The rat had screamed in ways she thought only people and ghosts could, but that had not stopped her as red stained over the lake's sandy shore.

Red and orange lakegulls hopped just out of her reach, squawking and looking for an easy meal of her science, their feathers ruffled by the wind which pulled at her black braid and tore the coloring leaves from the trees around her.

Then the stomach, the scraps of corn and rice Saumi's mother had thrown out the night before, still digesting. Then the six pink blobs squirming about the uterus. Saumi had tried to cut open one of those blobs, to see if it would look like its mother, but her knife was too indelicate.

The rat had died quickly—as would the hundreds of other small animals she would later study—but she remembered this first rat perfectly, the digesting rice and slowing heart, for that was the moment Saumi knew she would give her life to the understanding of the body.

1856 A.Y. Noav 20

"Her heart rate is holding steady between one-twenty-two and one-twenty-five." A voice, far, far away. Familiar.

Pain beyond identity. An internal burning. The tearing of the body on a cellular level. An impaling of the cell membrane and straight to the nucleus.

"The virus is spreading too quickly."

"Too quickly?"

Gray and white walls. Bright red lights visible through blurred vision. A hard bed. Black straps. Screams.

"Well, not too quickly, just... any faster and she'll die. The body can't handle physical change this fast without cellular repair. If the virus keeps delivering the mutagens before a majority of the already changing cells have time to repa—"

"I know how it works."

The unraveling of the DNA. A stripping. A deconstructing, then reworking. A puzzle fitting and refitting and replacing and refitting again.

"The gills are starting to form."

"Already?"

"Look, see here, and here."

"By the Four's tits, I swear if we lose her, I will fire all of you!"

The Four? The Four, again familiar. But pain, unzipping and restitching the secret to life, the heart beat, and breath. A scream, throat yelled raw.

"Ah, she's not so important. We already have thirty successful mutants, and as long as those living in the Rack keep popping out babies, we'll always have more to test on."

"Dr. Josto, this is your colleague, not some half starved child from the Rack. I swear if you don't keep those useless thoughts to yourself, you'll be on this table screaming next, and when the transformation's done, you won't be going to the tanks. By the Four, I'll have you on that table over there."

"The dissection table?"

"Yes!" A sigh. "I can't believe you were the best we could find."

A throaty laugh. "Well, you don't exactly have a line of Nomstro graduates to pick from. If questions of morality don't turn someone away, then the possibility of life in prison might."

"And yet, here we are."

"Yes, Dr. Yetinmyer, here we are."

~~~

1856 A.Y. Noav 12

The lab was clean, just as Saumi Yanj liked it. The excrement had been mopped up, the body—deformed during its incomplete mutation—disposed of, the straps rolled up, and every surface wiped clean of dust and blood.
~~~

Pinned up to the white and gray wall were detailed charts of the successful mutants. They mapped the body's changes as the virus carried the mutagens throughout the test subject, rewriting the DNA of a person to become more adaptable to life under water, both fresh and salty like the cradle fish that swam up river each year.

A massive tank of water contained sensors hooked up to several computers, ready to record the conditions of a test subject that would never come. Saumi had been hopeful for this one. She had saved the young boy with patched up knees from the city-guard after he had stolen peaches from the orchard of some high end entrepreneur who had likely never even tasted the fruit from his trees.

Saumi had let him hide in her apartment as the guards passed, and had enticed him with more food than he would ever eat.

"I know somewhere where you'll never go hungry again." And that would have been true if he had survived the mutation.

She left the lab, looking up at the cutout image of the tusked whale taped above the door where Dr. Baylerd Josto had thought it would be amusing.

"One day our creations will be swimming and living right alongside those monsters." Dr. Josto had laughed, throwing a toned arm around Saumi and tugging at her black braid.

Saumi had never liked Dr. Josto. Dr. Josto was a man in his mid forties who acted as if he was one of Ressin's sculptures come to life to bless the women of this world. Beneath his lab coat, his yellow shirts—always yellow—were a bit too tight around his well toned chest and Saumi saw him flexing in the reflection of the glass at least once a day.

Shrugging off his arm, Saumi had looked to Dr. Yetinmyer who frowned and just shook her head.

Dr. Yetinmyer had run a dark hand over her tightly curled hair, pulled back into a severe bun, then said. "I doubt any of these test subjects will ever see the open ocean. Maybe their great grandchildren will, but we have a great deal more work to do before they're ready for that."

"I don't know." Dr. Josto had laughed, his blue eyes sparkling as he looked between Saumi and Dr. Yetinmyer. "We've done enough for them. I say let nature do the rest. Can you imagine a shark biting one of them in half?"

"Sharks don't go after people. We don't have enough caloric value to be worth their time." Dr. Yetinmyer had turned to her paperwork. "And our genetic engineering isn't going to change that."

Saumi sat on a bench before the aquarium, a faint reflection of herself staring back from the glass wall.

Following Dr. Yetinmyer's own design, a network of tubes and grated vents allowed water to flow freely between the ocean and the tank while keeping her—their—creations in. Their creations were people genetically mutated with adaptations to help them survive ever changing aquatic environments. Expandable ribcages to withstand the pressures of the deep. Reshaped cones within their eyes for focused vision under water. Gills along the rib cage, filtering air from the water into the lungs. Webbed fingers and toes. Those were the planned mutations, and, as Dr. Yetinmyer had predicted, the bodies of their creations had narrowed out from the endless swimming, despite the added layer of densely packed blubber.

But some mutations no one had expected. The colorful skin, different for every subject. The balding along the sides of the head, leaving only a knuckle-thick strip of hair running from the top of the forehead to the back of the neck. The long, thin tail that reminded Saumi of the monkeys that lived beyond the mountains.

Saumi liked the unexpected look of their creations, and she admired them now as they swam about the tank. Several of the younger subjects chased one another, while the older ones swam in endless circles or floated above the rocks, using their tails and hands in the fluid sign language they had developed. Saumi supposed the subjects were still people, and people would always have the need for communication.

Dr. Yetinmyer theorized that the language was a blend of regional sign languages likely used by the three deaf children they had tested on. Despite her attempts to learn, Dr. Yetinmyer could not break into the language. Saumi had tried learning as well, with just as little success. Watching, Saumi's eyes wandered to her favorite subject—a deep blue man with purple stripes along his chest—as his fingers shaped the words she did not know.

She had brought him here, a young man living on the streets with a baby. She had been more interested in the baby, for, surprisingly, babies were hard to come by, but his generous smile and quick laughter had grabbed her attention.

Saumi had let them live in her apartment for two weeks before bringing them to the lab, and in those weeks, she had found pleasure with him under the blankets on her couch. She had never let him into her bed—he had never asked—and when she knew she could not delay any longer, she had drugged him and left them in Dr. Yetinmyer's care. She had called out sick the following days, though the look in Dr. Yetinmyer's eyes told Saumi she was not fooled. When she returned, both the man and the baby had joined the tank of survivors.

"Do you think they remember life before mutation?" Dr. Josto had asked in one of his rare moments of contemplation, flexing as he adjusted the wave of his golden hair and stroked his trimmed beard.

"If you paid more attention to Dr. Coe's research instead of her ass, maybe you would remember that most of their memories return three to five weeks after the transformation." Dr. Yetinmyer had frowned, looking at him out of the side of her dark eyes.

"Well, these subjects, their memories?" Dr. Josto had wiped his mouth on the sleeve of his lab coat. "Do you think they remember that—"

"That your little bit of manhood is as unimpressive as your intelligence. Oh, they'll remember." Dr. Yetinmyer nodded.

Saumi watched as a small, bright green girl settled up against the blue man's back, her small arms wrapping around his shoulders. His daughter. The blue man smiled and reached back to stroke her head for a moment before continuing his conversation with an orange skinned man.

She remembered holding the infant girl on her lap, feeding her milk and singing nonsense songs. Saumi had learned neither the name of the blue man nor his daughter; names meant attachment, and attachment meant bad science. But bad science had not stopped her from—in her own mind—calling the girl Hwasa instead of Subject Twenty-Three.

Hwasa was far too young to remember her, but Saumi often found the blue man staring at her through the glass. Did he hate her? He should probably thank her; this life—where they were fed and cared for—was a thousand times better than dying in the Rack.

Leaving the conversation, the blue man swam his daughter to the surface where he threw her out of the water. Hwasa came splashing down, laughing amongst a waterfall of bubbles. Saumi wondered how much laughter Hwasa would have known living on the streets.

"Dr. Yanj?" Dr. Yetinmyer's voice echoed throughout the observation lab. "I didn't realize you were still here."

"Just watching." Saumi looked at Dr. Yetinmyer's reflection in the glass, her tightly curled hair pulled back into a severe bun. "They're beautiful."

"It's a good scientist who can take the time to appreciate the beauty of their work. It's amazing what we can do." Dr. Yetinmyer came to stand beside her, a soft smile in her eyes. "This science, it makes gods of us."

Saumi's stomach clenched briefly as she nodded. Then, after a moment, she asked. "Do you ever wonder who these people were before us? What their lives were like? You've seen the streets of the Rack. Starvation, drugs, children sold for sex, rotting bodies. That's no life. That's not even survival."

A brief pause. "You've done great things, Dr. Yanj. I'm proud to have you on the team."

Saumi hadn't talked to her parents since the day after her graduation from Osvore University, but even before then, her parents had never told her they were proud of her—"Pride was for the unbelievers."

"I am grateful for the opportunity to be here."

Dr. Yetinmyer smiled, then yawned. "I could stay here all night, but it's time to lock up. My bed is waiting and the morning is too close for my liking."

~~~

1856 A.Y. Noav 21

The world was in pain receding too slowly. Wet, almost cold. She could feel the ground beneath her feet, yet never the weight of herself against it. Something brushed against her neck. Something pinched at the crook of her arms. Something held her ankles and wrists. She jolted awake, eyes wide, heart racing, unable to make sense of what she saw: a bright orange body reflected in the glass, bound up like an X. From behind the naked body—a female body, her body —grew a long thin tail.
~~~

She screamed; water rushing down her throat and painfully pushing out the sides of her rib cage. Panic, she should be choking.

"Help!" But no sound came out.

Through the reflection of herself, she could see shapes—people—moving behind the glass.

"Help!" She pulled at the straps and felt pain in her elbows—her bright orange elbows. There, needles fed into red tubes, connected to a monitor where a tall dark skinned woman was typing.

How had she gotten here? How could she breathe? How could she see so clearly under the water?

The monitor beeped, and slowly she felt herself calming as she drifted in and out of awareness. Somewhere memories of drinking and laughter nagged at her mind.

~~~

1853 A.Y. Jubem 16

Saumi had met Dr. Graylin Yetinmyer during her final year at Osvore University. Dr. Yetinmyer had been guest professor in the Biology and Genetic Engineering Department and Saumi had taken every class Dr. Yetinmyer had offered, falling in love with her vision of people becoming their own gods and leading the world into next stages of evolution.

Dr. Yetinmyer was a precise woman, who, though somewhere in her late sixties, had the posture of a young noble, and looked strong enough to tear a tree in half. She had eyes that could cripple nations, and was so tall that her bun
~~~

would often snag one of the lower hanging lights over the lab tables.

"Even if the gods are out there, they're too busy shagging or pissing on one another's doorsteps to care about our prayers."

They had been sitting by the window in Dr. Yetinmyer's office, overlooking the courtyard where students sat on blankets, talking and doing homework.

Saumi had never heard anyone talk that way before, not in a nation where the Law of the Four was all powerful. Her parents would have denounced that sentiment until their last breath. Once her parents had supported her excitement for science; she remembered the pride on her father's face as he gave her her first anatomy book and told her to go explore the wonders of the world for herself. But as her parents had become more and more indoctrinated in the Faith of the Four, their rejection of science grew. When she applied to university, they had begged her to study literature or history, even math—anything but real science. They had even refused to attend her graduation later that year, her now-oh-so-holy father saying he could not condone or show support for the studies of demons.

"But you gave me my love for science!" Saumi had almost yelled at her parents when they had cut her school funding. "Now this religious obsession is brainwashing you. You cling to the Four just like our leaders cling to the power your blind faith gives them. But look at all the other nations, they've let go of their religious bonds and have found freedom in science, reality, and truth."

"And those other nations will one day suffer the wrath of the Gods." Her mother had been shaking. "The Four gave us this world not to understand, but to live in." Those words had stung, but science was life. That day, in Dr. Yetinmyer's office, Saumi's mind had expanded from the desire to understand to the desire to change, to guide, to becoming a god herself.

"Look at them down there, brilliant minds wasted. We as a society are too addicted to our fear of "wrongness" to ever do anything great. But just imagine what we could do if we looked past the ideas of 'right' and 'wrong' to the greater possibilities at our fingertips."

Dr. Yetinmyer had started pacing about her office—spectacularly clean—and looked at Saumi. "I need someone willing to take those risks. I need someone who is not afraid of being wrong."

That day, Saumi sold her heart to Dr. Yetinmyer's vision. She even wrote, *We are too afraid of being 'wrong' to ever do anything great,* in big characters on her dorm wall. The phrase became her mantra, and her roommate said that she even repeated it in her sleep.

After graduation—which her parents had blatantly not attended—Dr. Yetinmyer had asked. "What are you willing to do for science?"

"Anything." She had answered before Dr. Yetinmyer had even finished.

"Anything?"

"Anything! I would face being wrong a hundred—a thousand times for the chance to do something great." Dr.

Yetinmyer looked at her for a long time, then laughed. "I might have just the job for you."

~~~

1856 A.Y. Noav 22

Slowly, the drugs wore off and she woke to find herself unbound and unneedled, though red marks circled her ankles and wrists. Restless, she floated in the dim glow of the tank while the world beyond the glass was dark. Breathing was coming more naturally to her: in through the mouth, out through the gills on the ribcage. She no longer panicked when she opened her eyes and found herself under water, but when the bright lights beyond the glass flickered on, she found her heart racing again.

What was she doing here? With orange skin, webbed fingers and toes, a tail—a tail!—it was...she could not bring forward the words so close on her tongue, it was not right. Beyond the glass, the shapes of people were moving again. The tall dark woman was writing on a large white board. The golden haired man threw his arm around a red haired assistant who cringed away from him. Other people were typing at monitors or looking over papers. Kicking up to the glass, she pressed her hands and face against its smoothness. She watched the woman at the whiteboard writing words too small to read from the tank. When the woman finished, she capped the pen and turned, a proud, almost kind light in her eyes as she looked towards the tank.

Betrayal, she thought, though she could not understand why she felt so. She did not know who these people were,
~~~

only that they kept her here. Anger filled her as she pounded against the glass.

Then the golden haired man looked up at her, a self-satisfied smirk plastered across his face, and she felt the desire to strangle him, to watch his pale face glow red beneath the water. She swam up and pushed against the grate that locked her in, only stopping when the first drops of her blood clouded the water. She swam in circles, her fists and feet frantically beating against the glass, mouth open in a silent scream.

The golden haired man just laughed, but then the tall woman slapped him on the back side of the head, shutting him up. Some of the other people smirked at him. She continued to rage and rage.

She had been shaped like them, but when she tried to remember that past life, she could only find flickering, half formed images. The clearest memory was of a woman speaking words she could almost hear.

"We love you. We may not agree with you or understand your obsess—your passion for science. But you will always be our daughter and we will always love you."

Why had she resented that?

Exhausted, she floated to the bottom of the tank, clinging to that memory. For hours the scientists worked beyond the glass, but eventually they left, flicking off the lab lights and leaving her alone with the reflection of herself in the dim glow of the tank wall. Staring at her reflection, this was her body now—webbed fingers and toes, tail, and all.

~~~
~~~

1856 A.Y. Noav 23

They must have drugged her again, for she had no recollection of being moved, but she woke to find herself in a small tank attached to the massive aquarium where the other water people swam. The other mutations.

Three scientists stood on a stone platform above her tank, some with clipboards, and the golden haired man knelt down over her grate, smirking at her. In a quick motion, she splashed up, soaking him.

Cursing, the man jerked back, his yellow shirt visible beneath his dripping white lab coat. The other scientists laughed and she wished she could laugh too, but she just glared up in satisfaction, baring her teeth. They were sharper now.

A grating noise vibrated through her small tank and the glass wall dividing her from the aquarium swung open. She knew this place somehow, familiar in a far off way, but she didn't move. The water was salty, with a hundred other smells and tastes she couldn't give name to. Starfish, barnacles, mussels, and sea anemones clung to the stone walls, and kelp grew from the stone floors. Beyond the massive glass wall, she could see more scientists watching her; the tall dark scientist hugged a notebook to her chest.

The other water people were watching her as well. After a long moment, a woman with dark green skin swam up to the door and held out a hand. She looked at the green woman, her strip of black hair woven back into three thin braids. After a moment, she took the woman's hand, and together they swam into the larger tank.

A school of fish swam past both her and the green woman, clouding around them before swimming on, sending tingles all along her side. Surprised, she looked at her sides then moved her webbed hands just above her waist without touching her skin. More tingles.

The woman seemed to understand this, moving her own hand along her side. Understanding dawned on her—lateral line—fish, their ability to sense other objects and movement in the water. But how did she know this?

Other water people swam or floated around the tank, some looking over at her, others turning their attention back to whatever had interested them before her coming. She saw a blue man with a bright green child clinging to his back. Familiar. She touched her own stomach, had she had a baby before this?

A memory. Her in a tree house, saying a name, Hwasa.

Another memory.

Her as a child. A man—father?—carrying her on his back. Above them, a high ceiling painted with images of the sky and four people—a man, a woman, a man, a woman—shaped together to make the image of one woman. Happiness with a hint of skepticism. The memory fled her mind, and again, she felt the ever present tingling at her side.

~~~

1844 A.Y. Jay 19

When Saumi's father was a child, his father had built him a tree house among the branches of the old oak in their backyard. Now, that tree house was Saumi's laboratory,
~~~

where she kept the bones from her dissections in neatly la-beled boxes on shelves. Often she would spend whole days up there, reading over her notes or reassembling rat skele-tons from memory—she loved the way that the hip bone fit into its socket.

"What do you do up there all day?"

"I'm praying." Saumi used to lie—but was not the seeking of knowledge the most holy act?

Her mother had never believed her, but had never ar-gued either.

By the time she was eleven, Saumi had a perfect under-standing of the bodies of kittens, gophers, fish, lake gulls, and rats. She had filled dozens of notebooks with detailed notes and drawings of her findings. By twelve, she dissected her first human fetus, a late-term miscarriage of her friend's sister. She had compared her careful notes to those in the books on the human body she had permanently checked out from the library.

When she had taken apart every bit of the fetus, carefully freeing the tiny skeleton from its flesh, she set the bones in their own box, cushioned by an old pillow case.

Saumi loved that fetus skull, even naming it Hwasa—beloved one. She often cradled it, imagining it as her own child that would one day grow up and follow in her footsteps to the glory of science.

She never knew what her parents did with her collection of bones—her precious Hwasa—but one day when she was sixteen, she found the tree house empty. She had stared and stared and stared at the empty shelves for what might have been hours before running to the lake shore to cry.

She did not know how long she had been gone, but as the sky faded into night and the colorful swirls of the galaxy's arms stretched above her, she returned home. Even the notebooks in her room were gone.

Her parents did not say anything to her, nor she to them, but later that night as she passed their door on her way down to the kitchen, she overheard their quiet voices. "Where did we go wrong, Rila? What did we do?" Her father's voice was raw. "I don't know. I don't know. I tried so hard to raise her in the Faith of the Four. But... but what if Father Olar is right and science is the work of demons. I never believed it, but look at

this. Have we let demons corrupt our daughter? What kind of monster does this?" She could not tell if her mother's voice conveyed disgust, anger, or sadness. Maybe all three.

"That monster you're talking of is our daughter."

"I know she is our daughter, I am the one who pushed her out. But Ko, are you blind, this is the skull of a human child. And these notes! She's recorded everything here. Her notes say it was from a miscarriage. And it's too small to be of any true born child."

Thoughts of Hwasa, her precious child, in the hands of her parents turned her stomach. "But, Ko, what happens when it is a true born child? And what happens when that child is still alive— just look at her notes. How many of these animals were alive when she cut them open?" Her mother paused, a shaky breath. "And yet, even while I look at this horror, all I can think of is, how do we protect Saumi? How do we keep her safe from... from this?"

Her father was silent for a long moment. "We can't allow this to continue. This... this... her love of science has gone too far. We can't let her go down this path. No matter how much we love her, the world out there will only ever see a..."

"A monster." Her mother finished.

"Yes... yes, you're right, we must stop this before she hurts someone... or herself. This passion is... it has gone too far."

"It's not passion, it's obsession... no, not even obsession. It's addiction. Look at all of this."

Saumi did not stay to hear the rest. She just tiptoed quietly back to her room, furious that her parents could not understand the beauty of what she had done. The body, the most marvelous of machines, the greatest of nature's wonders.

"We must stop this." Her father's words echoed in her mind. Blood racing, she lay on her bed and cried into her pillow.

~~~

1856 A.Y. Noav 26

Days passed, and slowly she began to understand the ways of the water people—sleeping half awake on the rocks with only the rise and fall of the tides to tell of time, the collecting and re-distributing of the food that the scientists gave them, the language of their tails and hands— this was the way of her new life.
~~~

Over time memories leaked back in small pieces, but never enough for her to truly make sense of them.

She was welcomed among the water people by all except the blue man with the purple stripes. He kept his distance from her, and only once did he ever sign to her. She had tried approaching his daughter, but he had pulled the green child behind him and signing [Monster.]—at least that's what she thought he had signed—[You stay away from us, you monster.]

~~~

1856 A.Y. Noav 19

In celebration of their thirtieth successful mutation, Dr. Yetinmyer had cancelled all non essential work for the day and cracked open several boxes full of hard ciders and wine. Someone had dimmed the lights and a few brave—or drunk—hearts had even cleared a space for dancing.

"It's a good day, yes." Dr. Yetinmyer came to sit beside Saumi, a glass of wine in one hand and an opened cider in the other. Her curly black hair had been freed from its bun and now clouded around her head.

"It is indeed."

"The work we're doing—that you're doing—it inspires me every day." Dr. Yetinmyer raised a glass of wine to Saumi, whose cheeks were already red from drink. "To your dedication and passion for science. I wish the whole world were like you; imagine what we could accomplish."

"This is all your doing." Saumi motioned around the lab, to the tank where the water people were swimming about, some watching the celebration.
~~~

"I couldn't do it without you." She took another sip, then shook her head. "If only I could get closer, become a part of it. Really see what it's like from the inside, the depth of it all. You know?"

"Become one of the water people?" Saumi saw the blue man at the window, watching her—or at least she imagined that he was. "But if you're in there, who will lead us? We can't do any of this without you."

"I know... I know." Dr. Yetinmyer sighed. "If only I could find a way, get someone I trust on the inside."

"Maybe we could train a few children from the Rack, teach them all of," she waved her hands around, "this and then they can be our eyes on the inside."

"I love the way you think! Maybe we could—But no," Dr. Yetinmyer smiled, holding up a finger. "Those are thoughts for another day. Forgive me, Dr. Yanj, we are here to celebrate, not work."

"No, no, I understand." Saumi finished her drink. "What we do here is amazing, world changing! It's hard not to talk about."

"You sound like an extension of myself." Dr. Yetinmyer took a sip of her own wine and looked over to where Dr. Josto was getting handsy with one of the not-so-sober assistants.

Dr. Josto's blue eyes met Saumi's, and for a moment he almost looked guilty, before meeting Dr. Yetinmyer's eyes, her lips tight. Saumi shook her head as she placed her empty bottle on the table and reached for another cider.

"No, Dr. Yanj, this one is yours." Dr. Yetinmyer thrust the bottle she was holding into Saumi's hands. "Um, the ones in that box are for Dr. Coe."

"Excuse me." Saumi laughed, pushing her hair behind her ear. "I didn't realize there was order to this chaos."

"Only for Dr. Coe, you...Her's is a special order." Dr. Yetinmyer leaned closer and patted Saumi's belly. "She just doesn't want people to know yet."

Saumi raised an eyebrow, smiling as she looked over to where Dr. Coe was laughing with several other of the assistants and scientists.

"To Dr. Rista Coe." Saumi lifted her cider and took a long drink. It was a little more bitter than she had expected, but just as delicious.

"To discovery and progress. To all those who have dedicated their lives to science." Dr. Yetinmyer raised her glass. "I am proud of you, Saumi. I've always needed someone like you to help me see the depth of our work."

Saumi smiled, oddly drowsy, and felt the sudden urge to hug Dr. Yetinmyer. The world seemed to grow farther and farther away, and all she was left with was the image of swimming alongside Dr. Yetinmyer.

11

Diviner - Matthew Spence

Sorin looked down at the parched, dry ground as the light from Hermes' parent star glared down on him. After a few minutes of waving and prodding with his sensor stick, he nodded in satisfaction as he bore its drill tip into the ground. "Viscosity rising," he said. "Good. Now to tap into the flow..."

The stick released a clear, capped tube into the ground. The surrounding villagers watched with appreciation as water flowed into it. When it was full, Sorin picked it up and put it into a meter.

"It's clear," he said, causing a smattering of cheers from the small group. "No metals or toxins."

"How long will it be good for?" their leader, who had hired him, asked. "The old wells were only solvent for about a local year before they gave out."

"It should be good for at least two or three," Sorin replied. "There also might be other veins that you might want to try tapping yourselves-most of these wells are connected, after all."

The leader sighed with relief. "This will solve our growing problems for at least the next season. We owe you."

"Just add it to my tab," Sorin replied. "I'm just a go-between between you and the water. You folks are the ones who do all the hard work."

After getting his pay in energy credits, Sorin got in his rover and drove off to his next destination. Work had picked up with new settlers coming in. There were a lot of people who had come to Hermes to extract its minerals, but hadn't counted on the heat, the two main sequence stars in the sky, or the fact that most of the planet's water was more than a mile underground and they had to import drills to get to it.

First, of course, they had to find it. That was where he came in. There was nothing magical about it, just a matter of finding the right molecular traces and tapping into them, but it was precise work that only half a lifetime of training could produce. Sorin's was a rare skill on any world, and he knew he was lucky to have it.

He ran into the pirates after his last job. Sorin realized that they must have been following him, and were after his gear more than him, whom they would have been happy to have left for dead in Hermes's sun-baked wastes. He wasn't totally unprepared—he tried holding them off with a sonic microwave suppressor that he carried, but there were four of them, and they caught him and held him down while they demanded his gear as "payment" for crossing "their" territory.

"Can't give it to you," he said.

Their leader, who was half Sorin's age but acted like he was older and tougher, cackled. "How you gonna stop us, old man?" he taunted. "What you got instead that's worth more?"

"Information," Sorin replied. "I can tell you where to find the next well, maybe several. Surely that's worth an old man's life?"

The leader grunted. "Why we need you when we got your gear? Meters are worth more'n their weight in brain matter, an' yours won't be worth much once it's splattered on the sands." The others laughed along with him.

"You won't need a meter," Sorin reminded him. "I can show you a map of where to go. I can even give you my credits; I can always make more at another job. You could control the water in this territory with it. Now, how about it?"

The leader must have had at least some sense of mercy, or maybe he didn't see Sorin as any more of a threat than a sand gnat. "Okay, old man. Give us the map. You gonna die out here anyways."

Sorin gave him a holographic scanner display, pointing out various locations. "It's all there," he said. "All the wells you could need."

The leader frowned, but then nodded. "Okay, boys, let 'im go. We got what we need, we gonna be rich. We gonna own this territory!"

They all cheered and took off in clouds of dust on their desert cycles. When they were gone, Sorin picked himself up and got back in his rover. He was thankful to be alive, knowing that he wouldn't see them again.

After all, the first target was underneath a territorial defense base. If they somehow made it past that, the next was in a hot magma cave, and the third was in a region inhabited by viper worms that squirmed out of their nests under any moving target. Good luck, Sorin thought sardonically as he drove off to his next job.

Because, he thought, theirs won't last much longer.

12

The Diary of Debasish Ghosh - Robert Owen

February 3rd, 2020

I woke up on the right side of the bed. My wife's name is Shweta. We had aloo puri for breakfast. I made my way outside the apartment to my car, a Toyota. My driver, Danish, was talkative. I read the paper, The Calcutta Telegraph, to avoid him.

We reached my office around eleven, I work in a nine-story building in the Salt Lake sector.

I am the Head of Human Resources for an insurance company. I have a secretary, her name is Pooja.

I told Pooja to hold all calls and cancel all meetings for the day, as I had an important task to complete for the Boss.

Around four, a middle-aged man in a shiny, too snug, pin-striped suit barged into my office, knocking Pooja aside as he did so.

"What the hell, Deb?" He jabbed a flabby finger in my face as he spoke. "Why did you cancel the interview with Vyas? Everyone knows he's the best salesman this side of Hyderabad. We've worked months to get him on the team. Why man? Why?"

"Mr. Deepak, sir, Debasish Ji is working on something top secret for the Boss, please come now. I will call Vyas Ji and rearrange." Pooja placated the pompous buffoon as she showed him the door.

"I'm the Head of Sales around here, I should be the one…be the one cancelling any interviews involving my department!"

"Take it up with the Boss." I slung back as my secretary succeeded in ushering him out. She pulled the door closed behind her.

I hate salesmen.

My cabin was quiet, peaceful. I read the internet.

At seven, I asked a peon to call for my driver. I reached home at eight. We had macher jhol for dinner.

I claimed a headache and went to bed at eleven. Shweta snuggled up to me under the cover. I rolled away.

I miss you my Rani, my heart belongs to you, always.

February 4th, 2020

I woke up on the right side of the bed. My wife's name is Swati. We had dal puri for breakfast. I made my way outside the apartment to my car, a Toyota. My driver, Danish, again talkative. Again, I read the paper, The Statesman, to avoid him.

We reached the office around eleven, I still work in the nine-story building in the Salt Lake sector.

I am the Head of Sales for an insurance company, I have a secretary, her name is Srilekha.

I told Srilekha to hold all calls and cancel all meetings for the day as I had an important task to complete for the Boss.

At noon, Srilekha apologetically put an important phone call through from a M. M. Vyas. I know him, I studied at La Martiniere with him when we were boys. "DG how are you doing? You told the Boss the good news yet? I handed my papers in, they wept when they realized I was moving to you guys. Let the good times roll!" The same old arrogant manner, and annoying mannerisms.

"Actually, the Boss did some digging into your background, he found out you're a fraud and we've withdrawn the offer. Don't call me again." I slammed down the receiver. I hate salesmen.

That petty act of revenge was many years and many lives in the making. I found myself experiencing joy again. I found myself experiencing something again. Around four, a lean, middle aged man with greying sideburns and wire glasses burst into my office, leaving Srilekha tumbling in his wake. He had biscuit crumbs stuck in his well-groomed moustache.

"What the hell Ghosh? We've been working for months to get Vyas on board and you cut him loose at the last hurdle?" He loomed over my desk, if he'd been a cartoon character, steam would have vented out of both ears, "The only reason you got this job over Deepak is because you said you could reel Vyas in. Now he's threatening to sue me for loss of earnings and defamation of character."

I reached up and flicked a crumb out of the moustache. He recoiled, shock battling with indignation for control of those haughty features.

"You're fired. Collect your things and get out." I could tell he wanted to add more, but he controlled himself in front of Srilekha, after all it wouldn't do for one of the great merchant clan to swear in front of the help.

I sauntered out from behind my desk, gave a lazy bow to the Boss, turned, and exited the cabin.

"Sir Ji, your things?" Srilekha caught my elbow as I was halfway across the ninth floor. I shrugged, what were they to me anyway, nothing of mine for sure. As I exited the elevator at the entrance lobby, I ripped off my tie and threw it in the wastepaper basket by reception. I ignored the perplexed looks from the junior staff and made my way to a chai stall I'd seen earlier by the entrance.

A nice chai, a rare day when there was something to savour. Even rarer when there was more than one thing to savour.

I spent the afternoon wandering between the multitude of fishing ponds that gave Salt Lake its name.

I reached home around eight. We had kosha mangsho for dinner.

I claimed a headache and went to bed at eleven. Swati undressed and snuggled up to me naked as a new-born under the cover. I rolled away.

I miss you my Rani, where are you?

February 5th, 2020

I woke up on the left side of the bed. Reflexively I made sure my diary was under the pillow. My wife is still Swati. We had poha, from a packet, for breakfast. I made my way outside the apartment to my car, a Nano. My driver, Raj, was sullen. A good thing as it turned out, the ride was far too bumpy for me to read.

When we reached the office, I had a headache from the constant bashing of my head on the ceiling of the car. It was the same office, third time in a row. That was unusual.

As I stepped out of the elevator on the ninth floor, Srilekha zipped across the floor and grabbed my elbow. "It's gone eleven-thirty, I stalled him for you. He's in a foul mood but stick to your guns. You're the best salesman we have, and you deserve that promotion."

I hate salesmen.

Srilekha adjusted my tie and smiled flirtatiously as she led me to the cabin that yesterday had been mine. Stencilled on the frosted glass of the door was *M. M. Vyas, Head of Sales.*

Stepping across the threshold, I saw the familiar figure of my nemesis pacing behind his desk as he spoke on a hands-free device of some sort. His dyed jet-black locks slicked back as usual, his toned body filling the tailored suit, and, as ever, gold cufflinks glinted from the sleeves of his Italian shirt.

After leaving me standing for five minutes he finished his call and turned to me, "You're late DG, take a seat."

I stared for a moment into the smarmy features of the man who had stolen my Rani on so many occasions, then

I launched a savage jab to his face. He fell back, his nose a fountain of crimson. A savage elation washed over me. Then, a disturbing flashback.

As I ran from the security peons outside, weaving my way through the street food vendors and their ramshackle stalls, I had an epiphany as I realised that the only way I could feel anything at all now was by hurting Vyas.

The overweight rent-a-cops had long given up by the time I stopped at a patch of land where yesterday I'd skipped stones across the placid surface of a pond. Today a derelict building earmarked for demolition occupied the plot. I double checked the address on the warning sign, there was no doubt it was the same.

From my accumulated experiences, I knew that this meant a bigger shift was on the way. My elation faded into the usual blank acceptance. I drifted around the Salt Lake blocks aimlessly, trying to match a myriad of memories to the scenes in front of me.

Around four a jeep marked Bidhannagar Police pulled up alongside me, a couple of khaki uniformed constables bundled me into the back.

I spent the rest of the afternoon in the charging area of Bidhannagar Station. I spent the evening in their lock-up. They fed me watery daal and stale rotis. I have no idea what time I fell asleep.

February 6th, 2020

I woke up on the right side of the bed. Reflexively I made sure my diary was under the pillow. My wife is Srilekha. She woke me with oral sex. I didn't stop her. Afterwards I rolled away. She asked me what was wrong, I told her I felt shame and guilt.

"You don't like making love with me anymore?" Saucer-wide eyes stared into mine, lips trembling as she spoke.

"It wasn't making love, I used you. I'm sorry but my heart belongs to another." She burst into tears and buried her head under a pillow. Another wave of shame and guilt washed over me. So, hurting others as well as Vyas managed to elicit a response in me. I wondered if I'd ever feel a positive emotion again, whether I could ever be a good man again.

I gathered some clothes and my diary before leaving the unfortunate Srilekha to her own pain. Grabbing what was clearly my jacket from the rack by the front door I sped out of the apartment.

The society elevator was out, and as I raced down the stairwell with its fractured concrete steps, it became evident that the building was more ramshackle than the last few days.

A two-wheeler was parked in my spot outside, a battered TVS. Rooting through the jacket pockets, I came up with the keys.

I took Circus Avenue, or whatever its name was today, until I reached the free for all that was Park Circus, that never seemed to alter at least. Heading out of the junction, I motored up Park Street until I saw the familiar gates of the cemetery.

This time there was no fee, no ticket wallahs on the gate, and the famous burial ground was an unkempt mess. In truth, I did not mind, I welcomed the added shade and privacy that would allow me to investigate my hunch in peace.

Sitting on the plinth of a brick mausoleum, the resting place of one Hindoo Stuart, I opened the diary flicking back to the relevant entries.

I was right, I'd been hurtling through this personal torment for over a year now. If I could believe the diary. If I could believe my senses.

February 3rd, 2019

Normal day at the office. Making good progress on the streaming platform, we should be able to tie up all the sites in one place. Forecast for advertising revenue was a plus, for sure I will get that spot on the board, says the Boss. It happened again on the way home today, I'm sure of it this time. I got Ramlal to stop the car on the street. I got out and examined the shop. I'm certain it was closer to the junction again today. I measured the steps from Standard Meat butchers to the Gariahat Road crossing, fifteen paces. I will check again tomorrow. Reached home a little late because of my experiment, I explained why to Rani. She burst out laughing, said I always had a crazy imagination, but she loves me anyway. We ordered biryani from Arsalan and settled for the night in front of the television, watching India's Got Talent.

February 4th, 2019

Good day at the office. Boss is incredibly pleased with our efforts. I got Ramlal to stop the car on the way home so I could complete my experiment. I measured the steps from Standard Meat to the Gariahat Road crossing, ten paces! I was right! I walked fifteen paces also and stopped outside a mom and pop tobacconist. I asked the uncle behind the counter how long he had the place, he replied thirty years! It sure looked old enough. I was so excited I babbled to Ramlal all the way home. He thought I was joking. "Sir I watched you yesterday, it was only ten paces then. The shop is where it always was. I've bought mutton from there myself. It was always there." When I got home, I told Rani of my great discovery, she patted me gently on the cheek, "Yes dear, that's what you said yesterday. Now don't be silly, you just forgot your measurements, that's all."

I pouted for a while, she came over and snuggled whilst I surfed the channels looking for Got Talent. "Where is that blasted Karan Johar show?" "India's Got Talent? That doesn't start till next month, laddoo." "We watched it last night whilst we ate the biryani!" "That was Big Boss and pizza, are you feeling alright, Deb?" I said maybe I had a fever and went for a lie-down. I checked yesterday's entry, and everything was as I said, what is going on? I put the diary back in its usual spot under my pillow. Am I going mad? Should I see a doctor? Is everyone lying?

February 5th, 2019?

Terrible! Terrible! Terrible! Oh god. Where to begin? The shop, yes, the shop. The outbound flyover was closed so we took a diversion back through the Gariahat Crossing and the butcher, the blasted butcher, was on the other side of the road! It was always on my left coming home at night, this time it was on my left going in the opposite direction. I made Ramlal stop. I spoke to the owner of the shop, he said they moved from across the road ten years ago when the landlord wanted to develop apartments at the old site. Old site? It was just there yesterday! I thought my mind was collapsing. I told Ramlal I was ill and to take me home. Rani would help. Rani always knows what to do.

I unlocked the door to our flat, and pondered what to say to my wife as I walked on in. On the sofa was Rani, naked. She was writhing on another man. I screamed and collapsed to the marble tiles.

"Oh shit!" Rani scrambled from the sofa, grabbing the simple kurta I had watched her put on a few hours before. "Oh god, you weren't meant to find out this way!"

"What? Find out what?"

I couldn't take much more, was anything real? Was anything what I thought?

"That she was leaving you for a real man, a proper breadwinner. A go-getter, not a loser like you Deb." The other man's voice was horrifyingly familiar. I looked up at the sweaty and ridiculously hirsute torso of my childhood nemesis, M. M. Vyas.

"Bapri! This can't be, you dumped this idiot for me, because he was such an ass. Always hazing us."

"He's promised to provide me everything I need. What with your job going so badly, I need someone who help me look after Ma," Rani's tone was determined, but she couldn't look me in the eye, gaze locked at her feet as she reached out a hand to her lover, "with dad passing we'll need a bigger place when she comes to live with us."

"What do you mean my job going badly? Your Dad passing? What nonsense is this?"

"God you're pathetic Deb, can't admit the software company is going down the drain, can't even remember his father-in-law has passed. No wonder she came to me." Vyas stood, proudly strutting his manliness. I was pleased to see I beat him on one thing at least.

I turned to my wife, pleading, "Rani, please, this isn't you. The woman I know would never do this to me."

Vyas didn't let her reply, "You don't know her at all, you pathetic little geek. She's ambitious and she's happy to hook up with the number one insurance salesman in the area."

Something snapped inside, "I hate salesmen!" I launched myself up from the floor straight at the beast of a man. I don't know where the strength came from, but I was on him before he could blink. I smashed him in the face, his nose crumpling into a purple fountain. He lost his footing and tumbled backwards over the arm of the sofa. As gravity propelled him towards the floor, the back of his head connected with the sharp edge of the dining table. Rani screamed and dived over the three-seater to tend the Salesman of the Year. "Oh god, you bastard! You killed him. He's bloody dead. You murderer!"

"What? No that can't be." I swung around the lumpen furniture; a huge puddle of crimson had spread out from Vyas's head. I reached down to check his pulse. Nothing. "Shit, I'll call an ambulance."

"Too late, you bloody bastard. Get out, get out! I curse the day I met you, I curse your very existence! Bastard! Get out!"

I scrambled out of the apartment, out of the block, and out onto the road. I wandered for hours, expecting white uniformed constables to descend on me at any moment, but it didn't happen. As night fell, I found myself taking shelter under a flyover. I flopped down on a discarded mattress and closed my eyes. I don't know when I passed out.

February 6th, 2019?

I woke up on my usual side of the bed, the half-light drifting through the curtains. I must get Rani to change the blind. Rani!

I jumped up in bed, earning a disgruntled groan from the sleeping figure next to me. My breathing relaxed and the pace of my heart slowed. It must have been a dream. What a horrible dream though. I felt under the pillow for my diary, it was there as always. I snuggled up to my wife.

"It's too early," an unfamiliar voice replied. I rolled my bed companion over, a strange face looked at me with sleepy eyes. I screamed and sat bolt upright, scrambling for the edge of the bed.

"What the hell, Deb? What's wrong? Did you dream about Vyas again?"

"What the hell! What the hell? Who the hell are you?"

"Only Nidhi, your wife of the last five years, you numb-skull...I couldn't read anymore after that, it was all too painful, too raw. Every day the same pattern, always some change, sometimes minor and sometimes major. Every day though. The calendar seemed to pass as normal but always a change, a new wife, or a new house, maybe a new job. New friends, new family. Two things remained the same though, my diary, always under my pillow, and there was always Vyas somewhere.

Rani was often with him in the early days, but I hadn't seen her for months and I'd given up looking for her. It was never my Rani anyway. So, was I cursed then? Had Rani cursed me? Surely though the weirdness had started before...I killed Vyas; the diary confirmed that. Why did the world change so? Am I just rotting in an asylum somewhere? Am I lost in a coma? I need to sleep on this.

February 7th, 2020

Srilekha. My wife is still Srilekha. She woke me with oral sex. I didn't stop her. Afterwards she rolled away with a chuckle, "I know you love that. Never fails to get you up in time for work. Pay me back in kind tonight." I felt less guilt after re-reading the diary. Still, I felt some shame to use someone I barely knew. Quick as a flash, which seemed indecent so early in the morning, she was out of bed, flinging the blinds open.

"Gah! Too bright woman!"

"Can't let you drop off again, you have a big day ahead of you, saving the world from flooding, Mister Chief Engineer. Gods, I can't believe you got the promotion." She squealed and jumped back onto the bed. My eyes finally adjusted to the daylight, and as they did so I noticed something peculiar. "

You dyed your hair blonde?" As I peered closer, it wasn't just the hair, her skin was alabaster white.

"Always making fun of my hair, and my skin colour. I can't help it if my great grandmother came over from London with the Marahanee Victoria and the other refugees." Srilekha was speaking perfect Bengali like a native of North Kolkata, the features were still those that I'd come to know, but it was as if someone had replaced the woman with a Scandinavian clone. It was disconcerting. "I'll never be good enough for my high-born prince." She gave a dramatic sigh and rolled back out of bed, heading for the washroom. "Up at eight, can't be late for Kanoria and Sons, 'cos they won't wait." She hummed as she disappeared. She reappeared a few minutes later wearing underwear and smelling of turmeric toothpaste.

"What were you singing?"

"As if you haven't heard it before, a thousand times. My little mantra to ward off the evil spirits of boredom at the most thrilling firm of accountants in the universe." She yanked me off the bed and propelled me to the bathroom, "Your turn, get a move on, or I'll have to take up singing full time to keep us in the luxury we're accustomed to."

My driver was Arun, the car was an electric BMW. I work for Iverson Steel and Engineering at a huge high rise on Chowringhee in the centre of the city. Amongst a forest of such high rises along the road, this one stood out like a soaring redwood. Tethered to the roof was a massive airship, the biggest I'd ever seen, not that in truth I'd ever seen many.

My office is on the thirtieth floor, my secretary is Pooja. It was good to see a familiar face. I'm the Chief Engineer of a global project to halt planetary warming and combat rising sea levels. We're remarkably successful. A prominent sign on the lobby for the executive floor proclaimed saviours of the Bharat Empire, whatever that is.

I told Pooja to hold my calls, she reminded me I had a personal life insurance appointment booked for four with Mr. Vyas, I cancelled. I spent the afternoon admiring the amazing view from my cabin window. There were European looking folks everywhere, most seemed to be wearing traditional ethnic wear. I reached home around eight, we were too busy in the bedroom to eat. I fell asleep in the early hours of the morning.

February 14th, 2020?

They don't stop coming. They keep hunting us. Day and night. I'm not sure of the date anymore, I'm holed up with Srilekha, Pooja, and some others in a fallout shelter beneath the Iverson building. In this world, old man Iverson had it built in the nineteen seventies for some reason. Lucky us, it wasn't there yesterday, and we lost Pooja to one of the roaming gangs with nowhere to hide. Who are these Farmers they keep babbling about as they haul folks away screaming? These goons are everywhere, all over the world, and the globe is burning. I'm sure I saw Vyas leading a troop of the bastards today. Ha! Srilekha just reminded me it's Valentine's Day. I don't think we'll be able to celebrate in public, though she seems keen to try. Not sure when we'll get a chance again. Or when I'll get a chance to write again.

February 20th, 2020?

Oh gods! Are we safe in here? Anywhere? Those things, those hideous devilish monstrosities, they keep coming and nothing can stop them. Tentacles, metallic talons, impossibly large mouths filled with row upon row of shark's teeth. The stuff of nightmares made flesh. At least now we know who the Farmers are. The bunker reappeared this morning, but it's only Srilekha and I left.

Civilization is gone, whole cities slaughtered by these things. Most people they cull, but I've seen them eat a few in front of the condemned, a horrible last rite of sorts. Is it torture? Have I been in hell all along? I'm turning the light off now, maybe they'll miss us. Srilekha and I will huddle together and pray, though I've lost track of which religions there are here. We can hope as well as pray, I guess.

February 29th, 2020?

The Farmers have gone. I haven't seen the demons for four days. Though each time I've woken up since, the Earth seems to have suffered some calamity or other.

Today is the first day the world has been stable enough to stay in one place, and the first time in days I've had access to writing tools. I'm sitting in the old boardroom on the thirty first floor of the Iverson Tower.

I'm the Mayor of a small township based around the high rises on Chowringhee, and this is my stateroom. Here we failed in our attempts to halt global warming and the world suffered catastrophic sea level rises. Most of Kolkata is flooded, the water is as high as the tenth floor of this building. On the thirtieth floor below, there is a ramshackle bridge stretching from my old cabin to the next skyscraper. Similar structures span out in a rickety web across all the nearby towers.

I'm told the low-lying cities across the planet suffered the same fate. Those who couldn't, or wouldn't, evacuate have tried to build civilizations amongst the crumbling edifices of capitalism. The fate of the rest of the globe I know less about. Srilekha is still with me, as she has been throughout all these horrible days. She is always hopeful, always brave, practical to a fault and always beautiful. She saved my life several times in the horror days. Today she is fair again, it seems quite random from day to day what her genetics will throw out. The person inside is always caring though, and always in love with me.

If it wasn't for the memory of Rani, maybe...I must finish writing, to conserve our limited power the lights will be switched off at nine. My order.

March 11th, 2020

The world is normal again. I woke up on the left-hand side of the bed with Srilekha performing oral sex on me. She really shouldn't, in her condition. I will be a father for the first time, anywhere.

I work a menial job as a data cruncher for the government owned telecom provider just off Chowringhee. Srilekha is a senior partner with H. S. Kanoria & Sons across town. We met for lunch at a Chinese restaurant on Park Street. She is a gentle soul and always seems content with me no matter what circumstance I find us in.

I think, I think...I could love her. I should move on from Rani.

The things I have experienced with Srilekha have eclipsed what went before. I saw Vyas on the Metro as I travelled home. He looked his usual self and I wondered what had made him use public transport. We nodded politely to each other in recognition and there was no animosity. Many people wore face masks, I'm not sure why. I reached home around eight. We ordered pizza and watched Saif Ali Khan's new thriller serial on a streaming service. Srilekha fell asleep in my arms. I want to stay here. I want to stay with this person. Maybe I've turned a corner, maybe I've grown. Could my luck have changed?

March 12th, 2020

I woke up in the middle of the bed, alone. She is gone. I am lost again. I found her photo on the wall wreathed in a lotus garland.

My driver, Ramlal of all people, found me crying downstairs. He told me I have done the same on many days in the year since she was killed crossing Seven Point Crossing on foot. He dropped me at my work and reminded me that God works in mysterious ways.

Incredibly, I'm back at the software campus in Salt Lake, at my original job. My real job. The boss is still pleased with the progress, we are due to go live in a couple of days. I was numb as he delivered the praise, he must have noticed as he asked if I'd tried the dating website he recommended. I locked myself in my cabin and tried to focus on the work. The routines were familiar still, but my mind wandered to Srilekha, and Rani.

Rani's social media page proclaimed that she was happily married to Vyas with two bouncing baby boys. Her snaps looked anything but happy.

I still hate salesmen.

At four, my mother rung, a shock, as to me she had been dead for seven years. I cried, a lot. She told me to pull myself together, as Indian men don't cry. Being alive hadn't changed her disposition much.

I reached home at eight carrying a bottle of Blender's Pride and a takeaway pizza. Ramlal gave me a hug and a pat on the back as I got down from the Toyota. I don't know when I passed out.

March 13th, 2020

I woke up on the right-hand side of the bed with a warm body next to me. The body clambered out of bed and dashed for the bedroom toilet. For five minutes or more came the stop start noises of retching and dry heaving. A cold panic overtook me, and I found myself paralysed with fear and longing, able to offer my suffering companion neither assistance nor solace. The door to the toilet opened and my eyes took a moment to adjust to the glare of a sodium bulb.

Rani, by god it was Rani.

She held her belly. "Well Mr. Ghosh, I am now certain you will have to use your new director's salary to buy us a bigger apartment."

"Are you sure it's mine?" She doubled up with laughter, which sent her back to the toilet for another round. Once she was done, she sat next to me on the bed and smirked.

"You're lucky I know your sense of humour Mister. Other, lesser, women would be calling their parents to take them home by now."

I stared into the lovely brown eyes that I had missed so long, "When was the last time you saw, Vyas?"

Her face darkened, "OK now that's a sick joke too far. You know perfectly well that two of us got onto his bike that day, and only one of us walked away alive. It's been five years but I'm still sensitive about it, so please don't play." I was too stunned to respond. "Seriously Deb, stop it. The cops never did a thing and that cut me up for a long time. They said it was an accident, but I'm telling you that truck drove straight for us. It was personal."

Tears started to flow, and my protective instincts kicked in as I folded her in my arms. Her next words chilled me to the bone, "I haven't told you this before, but I cursed the driver. I was so angry." She shook within my grip, "My mother knows some old black magic and she taught me to lay down a dark curse that would haunt a man forever. For eternity. I spat that at the driver as he sped off. I hope he got what he deserved."

The world around me started to spin, but I forced the whirl of emotions down. "Listen, I'm going to take the day off and spend it with you, it isn't every day you learn you're starting a family. I'm going to spend it right here with you."

She blinked back some of the moisture from her eyes. "Are you sure? What about work?"

"I'm a director now. Apparently. I think it's time I called some shots. I don't ever want to miss this day." The rest of the day was beautiful, one of the finest of my lives. I know this though, whatever happens tomorrow, whether I wake up here or elsewhere this is the last diary entry. If all is well,

I'll put this childish thing in an incinerator. If the worst occurs, well then, let's just say I'll end my travails in my own way. Whatever transgressions I may, or may not, have occurred somewhere or somewhen, I've suffered enough. I can't go forward mourning two women. I can't, I just can't.

13

A Glimmer of Hope - Ace Rhodes

The first large-scale Mars mission to inhabit the planet took place nearly two years ago. The launch was successful, and the landing, even the first supply ship the colony received a few months *after* landing. Then, 5 months ago, all communication with Earth suddenly ended and has yet to be restored.

At first the colonists, composed of some of the best and brightest Earth had to offer, rigorously checked their own equipment in hopes of isolating the problem. However, it soon became clear the problem hadn't come from there end.

And so the colony has sat alone and isolated on the red planet until 2 days ago...

The colony's central hub, usually a place of scientific discussion and camaraderie, was now a battleground of dissenting voices.

Saya stood amidst the chaos, her heart pounding with the urgency of their situation. The topic of debate: whether to send a team to investigate the mysterious UFO that had appeared, hovering over the nearest plateau of Olympus Mons a day and a half earlier.

"We have no time for this!" Dr. Alan Whitaker, one of the lead engineers, said loudly, his face flushed with frustration. "Our priority should be identifying and combating the pathogen that's killing us."

"But what if the UFO holds the key to our survival?" Saya countered, her voice rising above the others. Her traditional Japanese-American parents had raised her to exude a temperament of quiet pride, but today she had to be loud.

"We cannot ignore this opportunity. We've lost contact with Earth, our supplies are dwindling, and this sickness is decimating our numbers. What else do we have to lose?"

In the time the colony had been on Mars, its fledgling population composed of scientists, engineers, and doctors—all pioneers in the quest to establish humanity's first foothold on the red planet, had become like family. But their mission had taken a dire turn months ago when all signals and communications with Earth had abruptly ceased. Fearing the worst, the colonists had begun thawing the infamous reddish-brown Martian soil to plant crops, only to discover a deadly sickness lurking within. The pathogen spread like wildfire, claiming lives within days after showing symptoms and leaving many more bedridden.

"I agree with Saya," Dr. Michelle Reynolds, a NASA engineer, chimed in. "The appearance of this UFO isn't a coincidence. We need to at least try to make contact. If there's even a slim chance they can help us, we have to take it."

Others in the room nodded, their faces marked by desperation and hope. But opposition remained.

"Why haven't they come to us then?" Dr. Whitaker persisted. "If they have the means to travel across the stars, why sit there, why not go a few miles more? Why wait for us to come to them?"

"Maybe they're assessing us, waiting to see if we're worth helping," Saya suggested. "Or maybe they're cautious, just like we are. Regardless, sitting here debating won't get us anywhere. We need action."

"And maybe they are testing a new biological weapon against us," Whitaker countered.

After hours of heated discussion, back and forth, a decision was finally made. Saya, along with Dr. Reynolds and a biologist named David Boyd, would take a rover and attempt the trip to the plateau of Olympus Mons. The plan was to take the rover as far as it could go and then make the ascent on foot. They knew the risks, but they had no choice.

As the hour of egress drew nearer, the team met at the mouth of the camp. The martian landscape stretched out before them, a vast, desolate expanse of red dust and rocky terrain. There, seeming to rise to the very heavens themselves stood the largest mountain in the solar system, Olympus Mons.

"At least it's not at the top I guess," David quipped. "Still, it's pretty imposing…"

They departed, trying to lose themselves and cover their fear with quips and conversation. The rover hummed as it traversed the rugged ground, carrying Saya, Michelle, and David toward the giant, still silver craft hovering over the lowest plateau of the mountain. Silence filled the cabin, each of them lost in their thoughts, the weight of their mission pressing down on them.

"Remember even though this whole trip is uphill, when we reach the rockier substrate, the pitch gets worse," Michelle said, breaking the silence. "From there, you'll have to continue on foot. Make sure your suits are sealed tight. I'll get the rover charged up for our return trip home."

Saya nodded, checking her suit's seals for the umpteenth time. She glanced at David, who was staring out the window, his face pale but determined. They had all been exposed to the pathogen to some degree, but the exact incubation period was unknown. One thing was for certain though...time was running out.

As they neared the base of rock, leaving the thick, sandier soil behind, the rover ironically began to struggle. This was no doubt because of the worsening incline and declination of battery power. Michelle was sweating and her nose began bleeding.

"Michelle!" David yelled. "Oh my god, what if we were wrong. She needs rest, maybe Whitaker was right, maybe we should have stayed and not split up our resources."

Though Saya started to speak, it was Michelle who reassured him, "No, we committed, David. Saya, you, and I are in this now. We made our choices knowing this could happen. And no matter what, we go all the way, yeah?"

Saya and David agreed, though it would be a lie to say the thoughts and doubts hadn't been with them since they left and would be with them to the end, whatever end that may be.

The team disembarked, David and Saya secured their helmets and oxygen packs, while Michelle began prepping the rover to transform into a solar recharging station. As the two climbed out, the ascent before them looked steep and treacherous, every step would be a battle against their own exhaustion.

What a battle it was, and if it weren't for the thin martian atmosphere and lower gravity, it would have been impossible.

Halfway up, disaster struck. Michelle came over the local comms. "I... I don't feel so good," she managed to say in a weakened voice. "If I don't answer, I may be asleep; I am exhausted all of a sudden, okay?"

Saya and David looked at one another, but it was clear—the sickness had taken hold.

"We can't stop now," Saya said, her voice trembling. "We're so close. We have to keep going."

David nodded, though his face was etched with worry. They continued in silence, promising themselves it would be alright. But as they climbed on, they began to feel the true weight of their reality.

A small while later, David tripped. He fell down the rocky crag side nearly 30 feet. Saya rushed as quickly as she could while keeping her footing the highest priority. As she neared him, she saw David attempt to stand and favor his right leg. Upon further inspection, and in addition to what appeared to be a severe strain, there seemed to be a tiny tear in the fabric of his suit somewhere, likely caused by the jagged rocks, allowing the thin, cold air to slowly seep in and his oxygen out.

"Go," David urged, his voice steadfast with resolve. "You have to finish this, Saya. For me, for them, for all of us."

With a heavy heart, Saya nodded and pressed on alone. The climb was brutal, each step a monumental effort. Her oxygen supply dwindled, her limbs screamed in protest, but she kept moving, driven by a fierce determination.

At last, she reached the plateau. The UFO stretched out before her, a sleek, otherworldly craft that seemed almost organic in its design. Her breath caught in her throat as the hatch slowly opened. A young boy, no more than ten years old, greeted her with a gentle smile.

"I mean you no harm," he said, his voice calm and soothing.

Saya blinked, struggling to comprehend. "Who... who are you?"

"I have taken this form so as not to frighten you," the boy explained. "We are here to help, as we are the only ones who now can."

Tears welled in Saya's eyes. "You know about Earth? What happened?"

"The asteroid was catastrophic," the boy said softly. "But your colony represents a... *continuation*. You value information, empathy, community, and courage. You and your small colony have demonstrated these qualities despite your great hardships and loss."

He handed her a vial of clear liquid. "This is the cure to the sickness that plagues your colony. If you communicate with your friends back at the colony, you may tell them they will find another vial they can replicate already waiting in your medical bay."

"H-how… you can *do* that?"

"In time, we will share many secrets. You are taking your first steps into a wider universe."

"Why are you doing this for us?"

"In the end, it was your courage and your conviction that pushed us finally to intercede."

Saya took the vial, a sense of awe and gratitude washing over her. "Thank you, thank you so much."

The boy smiled. "Go. Go back to your colony. Help them rebuild. And remember, the universe looks on."

As Saya made her way back down the plateau, she felt a renewed sense of purpose. The climb was still arduous, but the weight of despair had lifted. When she reached David, she found him unconscious but alive. With the antidote in hand, she administered it to him and then to Michelle.

Together, they made their way back to the rover and returned to the colony. The news of the antidote spread quickly, bringing a glimmer of hope to the beleaguered colonists. As they administered the cure, they watched in awe as the UFO slowly lifted off, fading from sight and becoming more and more opaque until it disappeared entirely.

Saya stood with her colleagues, feeling a deep sense of gratitude and pride. They had faced insurmountable odds and emerged victorious. Even as she looked out at the harsh, bleak landscaped isolation of Mars, she felt an overwhelming sense of gratitude, humility and hope—hope that they could build a new future, one defined by courage, community, and the enduring spirit of humanity.

14

The End Of The Highway - Mark Salzwedel

At the beginning of that particular wake cycle, I bathed in a tidal wave of relief and release—the anticipated spring after ten years of cold darkness traveling from 202 Aquarii out to the frontier,to TRAPPIST-1.

I sensed it in my body, from the ends of my too-long toenails to the tips of my kinky blond hair. The cybernetic eyes that replaced my useless ones two decades ago when I turned eighteen registered nothing amiss. I wondered if I was acquiring an allergy to something—any one of a thousand culprits in the air we all inhaled that circulated through every compartment along the horizon-busting length of our vast paving ship, the Stela. Last month, Dew, our overly tattooed medic, narrowed my last outbreak of sneezing and itchy eyes down to toluene or munch grass pollen.

Despite that, space travel was the most comfortable environment for an albino like me. I burned too easily on any planet warm enough to be comfortable. I rolled out of my bunk and slipped into a long phase-sleeve-type shirt I hadn't worn in almost a year. I liked the way it shimmered when I moved and drew attention away from my abnormally pale skin.

I hopped over to the latrine. It wasn't until the buzz of the depilator ceased its hunting and trimming of the whisker ends on my chin and upper lip that I realized that the change wasn't an addition. It was a deletion. The nearly constant rumbling and vibration of the main engines had decreased to a barely perceptible hum. We were decelerating more slowly, and I was getting lighter. We were approaching the end of the highway. We had spent the past ten years laying down a 3-light-year path of pellet fuel and navigation/communication buoys so that later ships could make the same trip in two weeks.

Reggie had warned us and said she would soon order us to move to one of the two habitat rings before we lost all acceleration and started free falling. On the way to the bridge, the elevator stopped, and she joined me.

"We have time for a meal before the main engines cut completely," Reggie said. She was an interesting mix of African, Asian, and Northern European roots, and when she dressed in a more flowing gown, it took me a moment to correct myself and remember that she was transitioning to becoming a he.

"I just want to check the buoy intervals to make sure we don't have to adjust the release of the last two," I mentioned.

"That is tied to shutting off the pellet distribution, not our speed, Win."

I hated to argue with the captain, but he was missing my point. "It doesn't matter if the pellets go beyond the end of the highway, if the buoys are too far apart, it may screw up nav computations."

"There's wiggle room there," he pointed out.

"I'd rather keep it as close as possible to equal spacing, if you don't object."

"Fine," he said, just as the elevator door opened in the galley. "Come back here when you're done. I want to meet with the shift crew."

He stepped off into the brightly lit galley. I caught just a glimpse of Dew and Kris at the table before the elevator door closed again. They didn't look in my direction. It was just as well.

Dew often called me Ghost because of my glowing eyes and albinism, and he had the reprehensible timing of doing that when Kris, our botanist, was around. I had been trying to befriend her for the entire trip, and his demeaning nick-name was his way of trying to establish a greater claim on Kris's attention.

Dew had an extensive head start. For the first five years, I was stuck out in front aboard the much smaller sweeper ship deflecting space rocks and sending back telemetry updates for most of each wake cycle. He and Kris had managed a brief affair in that time, but it had exhausted itself before the Stela started deceleration.

When the door slid open again, I stepped out onto the bridge. I knew the main engines were powering down quickly, because I leapt when I hadn't intended to as I approached the main console. So much of the upright display across the wide, arching console was blinking and refreshing simulations. Most of the ship's navigation was handled by computers. I found the log of the last three buoy releases and dragged them over to the nav panel. I needed to pull in the deceleration curve as well, and then the release point of the last pair of buoys fell into place.

I verified the computer's assumptions and had just turned toward the elevator when the red flashing lights and the blooping of the proximity alarm began.

I turned and headed back to the console to pull up the braking-end camera feed. It looked like a large asteroid was on an angular collision course too far from the Stela's waning exhaust cone to be deflected or burned up by it. I quickly tried to estimate with a mind that was still trying to fully awaken whether slowing our massive paving ship down or speeding it up would lead to less damage.

Without fully recognizing my conclusion, my hand reached for the main drive controls and increased their output so the Stela would, with fortune smiling on us, stop short of the asteroid's intersecting path. The computer advised me to take cover further back in the ship, in case the asteroid grazed the bridge. I was already recalculating our vectors when the asteroid performed a maneuver that disobeyed Newton's First Law. I pulled up the camera again. The dark shadow of the asteroid had changed direction and was in the process of heading beneath the Stela's flight path instead of into it.

I double-checked everything. There was no object or force I knew of that could have deflected the asteroid. It was protocol to let the braking drive clear objects on the second half of the trip, but I was on call for angular approaches like that one. I usually had enough advance warning to launch the sweeper ship and use the repulsors, but this object seemed to come out of nowhere, which was also unusual. I rewound the radar track to see why the computer hadn't flagged it earlier. I couldn't see where it had come from. Even so close to TRAPPIST-1 and with my enhanced vision, I couldn't pick black rocks like that out of the blackness of space. We relied almost exclusively on our radar.

The possibility of that asteroid being the leading edge of a field impelled me to refresh the long-range radar next. I extended the range to a million kilometers with a wider ninety-degree forward cone. I watched the signals return, and in a matter of days, we would pass by a large planet. It was too far from the star, according to the survey map Namama Corp had furnished. And it appeared to be surrounded by about a dozen other asteroids similar in size and configuration to the one that had nearly missed us.

As the strange asteroid passed under us, I ran a spectrographic scan on it. It came back with a very odd mixture of hard and soft metals for an asteroid: titanium, iron, phosphorus, cesium, and mercury. And it appeared to be emitting hydrocarbons.

I recalculated the release of the last two buoys given our slower approach to TRAPPIST-1 and changed the proximity sensors to pick up objects smaller and farther away before heading to the galley. When the elevator door opened there again, Reggie, Kris, and Dew were all sitting at the table eating.

"Where's Fafa?" I called out as I approached. My co-pilot was part of alpha shift too.

Dew didn't even look up from his food when he answered. "She had a malfunction in one of her cybernetics. I gave her a NumNum and told her to lie down for a while. Kris was gonna check if it had to be replaced after breakfast."

"I'll brief her after I finish with you guys," Reggie announced. "Have a seat, Win."

"I'm going to get some stim-juice and a bar first," I countered. He was a bit more of a micro-manager than I could tolerate for long stretches. Often, I had to abandon him and take refuge in some random other part of the ship.

Everyone remained calmly eating until I sat down with them. Kris spoke first. "I heard the proximity alarm go off, but then it ended before we could scramble. Was it a glitch?"

"I took care of it." I decided to let the full explanation wait until Reggie's briefing was over.

Reggie finished the last of whatever he was drinking. "At the rate I seem to be losing weight, we'll need to wake beta shift and transfer everyone to the braking-end habitat ring.

Getting that activated is your first priority Kris, before you help Fafa. Everyone else, move your stuff and then start activating systems there. Dew and Kris you're dismissed. Win, stay here with me for a minute."

The tall, Asian medic stood up from his chair and pressed a contact at his wrist. Suddenly his shirt became transparent to show off his tattoos and the definition in his more conventionally formed and pigmented muscles. It reminded me of a peacock. Kris glanced over in his direction and then turned away in disgust as she shuffled toward the elevator.

Reggie watched them leave and then casually said in a lower tone than usual, "I've been tracking our progress, and I was wondering why you interrupted the power-down cycle. That's going to add almost a week to our trip." Reggie and Dew had both installed brain leashes, which allowed them to screen out any type of emotions they didn't want to experience. Another captain without such an implant would probably have been chewing me out at that point.

"We were about to collide with an asteroid," I replied. "It seemed prudent."

"The limited duration of the increased burn didn't slow us that much, and I didn't feel any collision," Reggie mentioned. "Perhaps you overreacted to a near miss?"

"It was only a near miss because the asteroid changed course." I focused on my bar and juice again. I tried to imagine whether he would resort to calling me a liar.

"It wasn't an asteroid then," Reggie calmly deduced.

I thought about his proposition. The short time I had viewed the other asteroids near the outer planet had not given me a good sense of their trajectories yet. "Then there was this little thing about an additional 3.9 Earth-mass planet that wasn't on the Namama survey. There were more similar asteroids in its vicinity."

"There is a j?" Reggie looked more curious than surprised that the survey had missed an entire eighth planet.

"There is a j," I confirmed. The Namama survey had also neglected to warn us about a comet's orbit intersecting our previous flight path and a greater degree of tilt to the target system's ecliptic, both of which I had had to compensate for.

"We didn't have sufficient time to do a more thorough survey," Reggie explained. "There was pressure from our board of directors to open a new system before the end of the century. We relied primarily on telescopic surveys."

"So what does Namama Corp say we should do in case we encounter an asteroid that isn't really an asteroid?"

Reggie stood up and dumped his breakfast waste in the recycling bin. "I am pretty sure that possibility was not in their risk analysis. That, the new planet, and the new delay in completing the warp highway will require us to initiate an entangled exchange."

For the most part, we shipped our messages using old-fashioned radio waves reflected along the line of buoys we trailed behind us, and they arrived at various points in settled space months to years after we completed the mission. In emergencies, when we needed an immediate response, the Stela and other long-distance ships were outfitted with an instantaneous communication alternative. My sister, who is a student physicist back on 202 Aquarii, tried to explain it to me once. It relied on the timed decoherence of thousands of pairs of entangled, separated quantum particles to communicate instantly across huge distances.

Because the Stela was nearly twenty-two kilometers long, and the entangled communication array was in the farther accelerating end of the ship, it took Reggie and me two hours to get to it. We were getting progressively lighter over the course of our journey, and by the time the elevator arrived at the communications array, we were in freefall. The main engines had stopped firing. We still had several days in which our momentum would carry us to the end of the new exit ramp at the TRAPPIST-1 system.

The radio transmissions could be accessed from anywhere on either ship, so it was my first time since touring the docked Stela over a decade earlier to visit the communications array. There was a fairly compact console right off the elevator with four fixed stools along its length. Reggie launched himself well past that console to a small room that bordered on being a booth. I followed not far behind him and tried to get a look at things inside from the doorway.

A large rectangular box was angled upward with a manual keyboard and, more oddly, an old-fashioned scanner for chip purchases at the nearest edge.

"We need to be terse and concise," Reggie advised as he entered an access code.

"What did you need me here for?" I asked him.

"You saw what happened," he replied. "You were there."

"You know what information is likely to evoke the most helpful response," I countered.

We settled on: MINOR DELAY. 8 PLANETS. ODD PHENOMS. INVESTIGATE? The little LED display at the bottom reported that the forty-nine characters we had chosen, if I had to personally pay for them, would have eaten up more than half my earnings for the mission. "How long should we wait? Should we come back?" I asked.

"I guess we're going slow enough now we could've calculated what time of day it was back on Namama," Reggie said as he leaned against the far wall. "But even if it's the middle of their night, someone must be notified when we send such a high-priority message."

His last statement sounded a little like a question, but I didn't work directly with Namama Corp like he did, so I had even less to offer such a conjecture. Before I could decline to initiate the complicated time-dilation calculations, a light at the top of the board flashed and then the screen scrolled our message up slightly to accommodate a new letter: Y.

~~~

The full name of the small sweeper ship I'd piloted for most of the first half of the journey was the SamArjani, which we usually shortened to just Sam. Because Stela sounded like a woman's name, most of the crew referred to the two ships as Sam and Stella.

And usually Fafa and I were the only ones riding in Sam. It had only two crash seats. The rest of the ship was all cargo space, food storage and production, air recyclers, repulsor reservoirs, and engines.
~~~

With Fafa still out of commission and Reggie having a background in theoretical science, he was the logical choice for the other seat on our unscheduled away mission. Kris helped me provision the ship for two weeks and advised me, "Don't take that long!"

The little ship zipped out of the massive docking bay doorway in Stella. It took me a moment to orient myself, but the eighth planet in the TRAPPIST-1 system was fortunately on a reasonable vector, and we were soon angling toward it.

We had another close encounter with an asteroid-like object on our way, and we slowed down to get a better look at it. As we started to approach it, the Sam was suddenly shaking as if the neighbors upstairs had turned up the bass on their music too loud.

"What's the origin of those waves?" I shouted in Reggie's direction.

"I can't get a fix!" Reggie shouted back. "Get us out of here!"

I fired up the thrusters again, and the shaking of every surface in the ship eventually faded to stillness. I put us on course again to orbit the planet. "Those space rocks keep getting more bizarre," I observed.

"Agreed," he said. He unstrapped himself from his chair and headed toward the latrine. He called back, "It's hard to imagine their behavior is random or spontaneous."

~~~

The planet, which we still referred to simply by its original IAU schema as "j," was massive and very cold. A probe
~~~

we sent down into the atmosphere registered a gravity just under three-and-a-half gees and an average surface temperature of one hundred twenty degrees below zero Celsius. Near its poles, even oxygen and nitrogen condensed into liquids. The probe continued to gather air and mineral samples, and it was unexpected to find so little water ice.

The biggest surprise, however, was when we slowly brought the ship down through the smog and saw extensive manufactured structures, some with long vertical tubes spouting bluish flames, lining many of the hydrocarbon lakes that dotted the landscape. They looked like half-melted ice cream castles.

"Can Sam land down there?" Reggie asked. He sounded almost as shocked as I felt.

"You've got to be joking," I began. "We're not talking about ruins of some long-gone civilization. They're in active use! Do you see those smokestacks?"

"I was just asking." I got the impression Reggie's brain leash was getting overwhelmed. "We volunteered to investigate, though, Win, and they . . ."

"They wouldn't fault us for turning back now," I interrupted. "We can assume those rocky things are their spaceships, the structures around the lakes below us are their homes. I don't think we have to go meet them. They could have an unhealthy appetite for us or at least assume we're hostile. Let's just go back!"

Reggie seemed to regain his composure. "I am not eager to be in a first-contact situation either. But I will get fired if I don't do a thorough risk assessment before bringing developers and eventually colonists to the inner planets. I need to find out if the neighbors are going to be . . . neighborly or not. We need to at least see what we're dealing with in person. They have enough technological knowledge to build manufacturing plants and send crafts into space. We can't afford to ignore them, especially if there's a chance we can coexist."

Sam wasn't constructed for landing anywhere but a space dock, but emergency landings were covered in my training. I double-checked the acceleration needed for escape velocity and reoriented the repulsors to slow our descent. "I'll look for an unoccupied stretch to set us down."

~~~

It took us over three days to orbit the planet twice. We chose a stretch of ground long enough for a landing strip and not too far from alien structures and made our descent.

Our spacesuits were rated for space walks, so their insulation was more than sufficient to protect us on the surface. I had worn one several times on our journey to TRAPPIST-1, but it looked like it had been a while since Reggie had. I double-checked his seals, and he didn't seem to consider the assistance too overbearing. The outer door of the airlock seemed to get stuck halfway open. Reggie was still biologically a woman and smaller, so I wasn't sure if it was that or him being the captain that convinced him I was the better candidate to manually push the hatch the rest of the way open. It was a little easier than I expected once the servos in the suit turned on.
~~~

It felt like stepping out into a winter's evening back home at the cottage on Mondu Tupper I shared with my sister. The sky was dark and cloudy, and the tiny, pinkish-orange TRAPPIST-1 star barely penetrated the haze. The ground was slippery, like slush on smooth rock, and it stained my boots orange. I could see the blue flame at the top of one of the smokestacks just beyond a nearby rise, and I pointed with the laser rifle I was carrying in that direction. Reggie nodded and started trudging up the slippery hill beside me. For a moment, I wondered if the servos in his suit were functioning, but then I decided he wouldn't have been able to move at all if not—weighing almost four times more than he was used to.

When we got to the top of the hill, Reggie was waving at me weakly. I realized I hadn't turned my helmet radio on yet. I initially heard Reggie almost out of breath, panting from the exertion even with his suit's assistance up the slight incline. I realized I probably got a lot more exercise than he did. "Do you need to rest?"

He was staring down into the valley before us and started pointing in the same direction. "Do you see them?"

I focused my cybernetic eyes to zoom in as close as I could. I saw huge, frost-covered snakes sliding like molasses out of round holes in the buildings. Other grayish-white snakes emerged from the hydrocarbon lakes like crocodiles taking their time to emerge from a swamp back on Mondu Tupper. And if their size, easily a meter or so in diameter, were not enough, the leading end of each creature terminated in a large mouth ringed with slowly fidgeting fingers of various lengths. When I noticed two of the creatures slowly, slowly entwining around each other, I noticed trapezoidal-shaped brown bumps along the sides of the snakes starting about two meters beyond their fingered mouths that seemed to lead their movement. "They look like big earthworms with fingers around their mouths at the front end," I replied.

"Those are fingers?" Reggie took a step closer and leaned forward. "You can see that detail from here?"

I replied to his second question. "I can read an e-pad screen fifty meters away."

Reggie seemed to be speaking to himself as he slowly backed away from the aliens. "Okay, we know what they look like, and they seem relatively harmless...I don't think we need to get any closer than this."

"We don't even know how they react to us yet," I argued. "What about your 'thorough risk assessment?'"

Reggie was already turned to head back to the ship. "Just don't contradict my report, and we'll be fine with Namama. We can always hold their sloppy survey over their heads, if we need to."

I watched one of their huge, ore-covered ships lift off just beyond the edge of the horizon and climb into the smog layer. I brought my gaze down to the aliens next and realized after watching them for a few minutes, that they didn't delay very long in coming out of their structures before they dove into the hydrocarbon lakes with their mouths wide open. After a couple of minutes, I followed Reggie down the hill toward Sam.

Because we slipped more than we stepped down the hill, we were watching our feet. By the time we got to the bottom of the hill, we were too low to see the top of Sam and whether anything was preparing to hitch a ride with us back to Stella. We noticed that the outer airlock hatch was still open and the inner airlock hatch was still closed. We noticed as we lifted off and tried to radio back that there was an unusual amount of static interference in the transmission. I made a mental note to check after we returned to the Stella whether the comm tower on top of Sam was damaged or blocked.

~~~

The trip back to Stella took only an hour, because the bigger ship was beginning to approach the planet just above its orbital path. But over the course of that hour, Sam was buffeted with upper atmospheric winds over a hundred kilometers per hour and almost two hundred degrees below zero, heated with the acceleration through the atmosphere, and then plunged into negative-three-hundred-degree interplanetary space with only the heat from its drive plume to offset the cold. Nothing clinging to the outside of Sam should have survived the trip. Something almost didn't.

We had to wait a few minutes after we landed again in Stella's docking bay for the hangar door to close. During that time, the temperature there was nearly the same as on the planet we had visited. I had flown Sam in and out of the hangar often, and I knew the exact amount of time it took for atmosphere and heat to reenter the docks after the door closed without having to stare at the gauges onboard. Af-
~~~

ter about twelve minutes, there was just enough atmosphere and heat that I could pop the hatch and jog to the elevator without losing any feeling in my ears, fingers, or toes. Reggie tried to lope along behind me, but he eventually gave up and trudged.

~~~

Several days later, the rest of the crew set about closing down Stella's systems to await a new crew of workers and a new stretch of warp highway that needed paving from TRAPPIST-1 to some other star system. I was helping Kris harvest and pack food to take with us on the two-week return trip in the medium-sized warp schooner we hadn't named yet. It was a little slow going in zero gees, but the corridors near the gardens were narrow enough and had plenty of handholds. Kris had grown addicted to the ground beef patties in one of Stella's freezers, and she launched herself off to snag some to load on the schooner as well.

Less than a minute later, I heard her scream. I let go of the armload of corn I was holding and grabbed a handhold to change direction. When I got to the freezer section, I saw Kris backed up a wall near the ceiling, staring in terror at the closed door to one of the freezer compartments.

"What happened?" I shouted as I approached.

"W-w-one of those things…" she began as she pointed an unsteady finger toward the freezer. "In there!"

I finally got close enough to her to grab onto her upper arm. She was trembling violently. "What did you see?"

"Huge . . . ugly . . . snake-thing," she eventually blurted out.
~~~

When I opened the door, my nostrils started burning. My artificial eyes couldn't miss the smaller, shorter alien coiled up on itself in the back by the fan grating between the two sets of shelves. I pinched my nose shut as I stepped through the doorway. All of the shelves and the door frame started vibrating. The creature was vibrating too.

"It seems scared," I commented as I backed out.

I had almost forgotten Kris was still cowering behind me. "I'm scared!"

I turned around and addressed her as calmly as I could. The compassion and understanding coming out of my mouth even seemed unnatural to me. As an albino of African descent growing up on Dewdrop Spa World 2, I had been the alien surrounded by equally scared people of more common pigmentations. I had learned to not see the differences.

"It's an immature alien. It's probably more scared of us, and it's probably close to dying. It probably hasn't eaten in a week, and it's probably not cold enough even in the freezer."

"Just close it and lock the door!" Kris urged me. My perspective had not eased her anxiety about a strange alien only a couple of meters away.

I sighed. After seeing the snake-like creatures briefly in their home environment, and seeing the marvels of their tech, I refused to believe they were dangerous. "We need to figure out how to feed it and get it to a colder environment. I'll be right back."

Before I could go, she shouted, "Don't leave me here with it!"

I grabbed onto a support beam to stop myself. My cybernetic eyes identified the irritating colorless gas as methane, and that gave me the idea that what I had originally conceived of as the aliens recreationally swimming in their hydrocarbon lakes was actually feeding. "Is there somewhere near here I could find some oil or petroleum?"

Kris directed me to a maintenance pod between freezers two and three, and there was indeed a canister of machine oil in it. I returned to Kris and the alien, in freezer one, with the oil. I leaned in toward the cowering alien snake and squirted a small quantity of the oil into the air between us.

The fingers around its mouth started twitching and reoriented itself toward the floating droplets of oil. It darted forward to consume the drops and then immediately pulled back toward the rear wall.

I left a larger slick of oil hanging in the air much closer to the freezer doorway. I motioned for Kris to move, and we both backed away from the doorway. A few seconds later, it had poked its many-fingered mouth out the doorway, as if it were checking to see if the coast was clear.

I told Kris to go alert the others, and I led the creature with ever-bigger snacks of oil into the docking bay. I made it to the control booth just as the rear end of the snake creature cleared the docking bay hatch. I opened the hangar door, and the temperature in the docks quickly decreased until the average temperature was around negative one-twenty. The alien had wrapped itself around a pylon to keep from being sucked out the gap in the slowly opening hangar door. I connected to the ship-wide intercom and announced that we were taking on an additional passenger for the trip back to 202 Aquarii, and we would need to provide special quarters.

Reggie intercepted me on my way to the habitat ring. "Do you really want me to dock your pay again?" he shouted.

I hadn't seen him coming, so I jumped a bit. Once I recovered and he came to a stop beside me, I replied, "What did I do wrong this time?"

"Really?" His sarcasm was fairly heavy. "You don't see anything wrong with unilaterally deciding to vent kiloliters of oxygen and thousands of joules of energy through heat dissipation? With bypassing chain of command and deciding the fate of a stowaway?"

I turned to face him, unable to hold my temper. "So you want to kill it? It has to be just a juvenile!"

"We have no idea what it's capable of," he calmly retorted.

"Whose fault is that?"

Reggie smoothed his tousled hair and massaged his temples for a moment. He sighed and then finally responded. "Do you even know how to care for it?"

~~~

Only one of the schooner's cargo holds was in the portion of the ship subject to centrifugal gee forces. Reggie even helped design and build the tank in that area to keep the creature's hydrocarbon bath at a constant one hundred and twenty degrees below zero. During the fortnight journey back along our brand new warp highway, I spent my breaks from piloting the nine of us back to watch the young
~~~

creature slowly growing a little fatter and longer. It writhed slowly as it floated, and the action seemed to loosen bits of its skin that accumulated in the bottom of the tank. Eventually tiny little white worms emerged from the sloughed skin at the bottom of the tank. I imagined the alien as a pregnant teen rebelling against overly strict parents, willing to do anything to get away.

After finishing my daily duties of refreshing the alien's bath and venting the accumulated methane, I dragged Reggie into the cargo hold, pointed at the baby worms, and shared my fantasy with him. The rest of the crew had headed to the galley to eat. "What do you think of that, Reggie?"

He smiled. "I can relate. That was me leaving New Earth. I had my first child on Salazar, my second child on New Tibet. I took them with me as I wandered the stars. The younger one died, and the older one left me to try his luck back at the casinos on Dewdrop Spa Planet 3. I decided to stop calling myself Regina when I got to 202 Aquarii. I haven't looked back at all that until tonight."

"I don't feel I can ever leave my difference behind," I told him. I thought about all the frightened and derisive looks I'd received wherever I went. "Even in a crew of nine I've known over ten years, I can't escape it. Dew still calls me Ghost when you're not around."

Reggie sighed. "Oh, I've heard it, and I think Mr. Duotek is a creatogenic and pornography addict with low self-esteem. I wouldn't worry too much about his opinion."

I noticed tears welling up in Reggie's eyes, and I tried not to stare. "Did you turn off your brain leash, Captain?"

Reggie carefully dabbed his eyes with the sleeve of his jacket. "I did. I realized I didn't have the compassion necessary to let that alien live and bring her along. I had suppressed every sadness neurotransmitter response in my profile. I can't keep walling myself off from what it is to be human."

We watched the white-colored alien with the brown cysts and her tiny brood twist and stretch in their tank a while longer. As we both got up to join the others in the galley, Reggie said, "I might even get a promotion for bringing a live alien back from the end of the highway for study."

"That's the Reggie I remember," I teased.

Reggie chuckled. "Yeah, that sentimental shite isn't really me, is it?"

I wondered if our runaway would ever want to go back to j. The way its fingered mouth-end seemed to follow me as I moved through the cargo bay, I got the feeling I would have to be the one to take it back. We didn't know if it could sense light or color, or if it was using some other sense to track my movements. I chose to imagine the young alien appreciating me as the only one of those little upright creatures with the right pigmentation.

15

Memory - C. Quinn

The login indicator for his game was boring. He was running seven other processes while he waited for the server handshake protocol to finish, including finishing up a movie from before The Fall. The latest upgrades to the network meant he had nearly limitless memory access. As the startup sequence for the game began, he actualized one of his current favorite avatars. He stepped into the game's lobby, a seven-foot tall, neon green version of himself—or at least as near to himself as he could remember. It had been so long since he checked, so long since he'd even thought of checking. Mirrors obviously were not an option anymore. But green was cool right now, or it was trending in the last several minutes at least. That was all anyone would really notice.

He had more than 90 avatars he could have chosen from. Crazy how several centuries will really flesh out your wardrobe. But it had been easy to pick this time. This game was usually played by younger beings, or at least beings that wanted to feel young and hip and woke. Or whatever the latest slang was circulating. He wanted to feel young and look cool. Set aside the centuries for a couple cycles and pretend to be a digital native. Fit in. It made things...easier. Some things never change.

In 2521, picking your avatar was about as fluid as the long-extinct chameleon's skin; you wore however you wanted to identify. Gender, race, sexuality and even identity itself was up for grabs—it wasn't like anyone could ever see you to call you out on it. The morons in 2109 had made sure of that. Nobody would be knocking on anyone's bunker doors. Nobody was even around to make the journey.

Growing up, "The Apocalypse" had always been hot, dusty, adventurous stories of wastelands; oft infested with robber barons and vagabonds and one lonely noble outlaw, finding his way.

The truth is always colder.

In fairness most of the old world was wasteland. But there wasn't much to be said for wandering around. The surface had been turned to so much ash and glass. Radiation didn't make the surface glow, not like in cartoons, but the chill air was no less deadly. It hardly mattered. The real glow was deep within, thermal generators humming to keep the databanks alive, and in doing so keeping the last of humanity...well, alive was one way of describing it.

In the decades leading up to The Fall, stories had circulated time and time again of how humanity would upload itself into the glorious singularity, becoming one with the machines they had designed and living forever. When the tech had finally caught up with the hype, that first wave of explorers had been uploaded almost overnight.

The state-sanctioned cyber-criminals who also went in that first upload were ruthlessly effective. There had been about 6 months of continual, systematic destruction as aged infrastructure was exploited repeatedly. After that point, the wheels of war were spinning and would not be stopped. As the geopolitical situation verged on apocalyptic, most private industry reshaped itself. The writing was on the wall. Like rats in a building on fire, the collective private industry sought a way to survive. The server farms built undersea were the first—the poor souls who uploaded into those backups became a stark lesson on the fragility of digital immortality.

One of the first measures of security a digital native now took was to secure backup hard storage in multiple locations. A series of server commands, a currency transaction. But only those beings who had been sentient before The Fall could truly understand what that security meant. How could you really explain to a digital native the concepts of concrete, immutable earth encasing the tiny components that kept everything running? Or how an earthquake along the wrong fault line could disconnect a vault from the grid and permanently erase anything not backed up?

He hadn't tried to have that conversation in longer than he could remember. Relationships were so transient now. You could step from one moment to the next an entirely different being, limited only by your whims and imagination. Digital natives took to it more naturally, having never known anything else. For some it was the ease of going with the flow, treading the path of least social resistance. For some, it begets opportunity for near-permanent hate. There was always something to discriminate against, always a fight to pick when you could change anything about yourself.

He died again. This new game was a little tricky, unfamiliar. He found himself losing interest. Four other processes were stimulating him, and he exited out of the game with little fanfare. No one would have noticed had he announced he was leaving. In the 14 minutes he'd been playing, he hadn't acknowledged any of the hundreds of players who had joined and left the game either. Instant gratification had taken on a fundamental role in the facsimile of lives now led.

However, it hadn't all faded away. On cycles like this one, when he was reminded that he couldn't even remember what he had once looked like, he retreated from the web. He severed each connection one at a time, viscerally feeling the shadow of a memory: turning off the lights one by one. Drawing the shades. Checking the locks on the doors.

He had survived The Fall. He had made his preparations with his own hands, could still tell himself that he remembered what having hands actually felt like. Somewhere in what had once been a mountain range on the continent of South America, there was a bunker system that he had helped design. Locked away in that long-forgotten vault was a room. He had taken painstaking care to develop his own fail-safes, his own recovery protocols. Backups upon backups, redundant battery systems, and of course extra memory.

It had taken up most of the space in that small chamber. Space had been at a premium, but he had known that the expense would be worth it. Most of the space, but not quite all. There had been enough extra room for an empty desk, bracketed by bookshelves. Still plugged into the bunker's systems, across from the desk and drawing barely any power at all, was a now-archaic webcam. It could only pan left or pan right. He had been forced to be strategic before he sealed it all away.

All of his processing power was available to him whenever he visited this ip address; devoted solely to this. He allowed no distractions—in a world where the thin line between life and death had been erased, this was the closest he came to a religious experience. This was his shrine, not to a nebulous deity or the promise of a brighter future but rather to the comfort of a past that could never again be.

He panned left. He took in a bookcase, carefully preserved so that the books encased there wouldn't rot away to nothing. Relics of an era before everything was so damn connected. Humanity's first crack at time travel. He'd walked with the greats, been enchanted by their minds, and pondered life's mysteries with scholars who lived thousands of years before he'd been born. Perhaps he'd ponder life's mysteries in real time with beings born thousands of years from now.

He panned right. Across a lifetime's worth of memorabilia, yet encompassing a meager fraction of the time he'd been "alive." A handful of trophies, from a time when trophies had meaning. A set of rings, the first two from schools and the latter a matched set that wouldn't ever again feel the warmth of promised hands. A violin he had bought in a pawn shop in Venice. Two ticket stubs to a Broadway show he had felt was a timeless classic. He could hardly remember the night.

Oh how things fade.

There in the center, a tarnished locket shaped like a heart. On the one side, a picture of his mother. A face he never forgot, no matter how long he spent on the net, no matter how split his focus became. The kind of anchor point that a being can always find. His north star.

On the other, a picture of himself, his arms wrapped around the last person he'd kissed. Immutable and therefore foreign to a world that could simulate every sensation without any reality at all. And yet all he had left of her.

He was awash in memory, in a way that only seemed to truly hit him as he immersed himself in the past. There was no need for immediate gratification in the contemplation of what had been. No need for multiple stimulating processes when the weight of your entire attention could be levied upon a scene and still find more to drink in.

He panned back and forth for a while longer. He wasn't sure how long he spent this time. The world had ended. He had all the time in the world to access this memory.

Although, he could have checked the log…